The Short Stories of Edith Wharton

Volume IV - The Muse's Tragedy & Other Stories

Edith Newbold Jones was born in New York on January 24, 1862. Born into wealth, this background of privilege gave her a wealth of experience to eventually, after several false starts, produce many works based on it culminating in her Pulitzer Prize winning novel 'The Age Of Innocence'

Marriage to Edward Robbins Wharton, who was 12 years older in 1885 seemed to offer much and for some years they travelled extensively. After some years it was apparent that her husband suffered from acute depression and so the travelling ceased and they retired to The Mount, their estate designed by Edith. By 1908 his condition was said to be incurable and prior to divorcing Edward in 1913 she began an affair, in 1908, with Morton Fullerton, a Times journalist, who was her intellectual equal and allowed her writing talents to push forward and write the novels for which she is so well known.

Acknowledged as one of the great American writers with novels such as Ethan Frome and the House of Mirth among many. Wharton also wrote many short stories, including ghost stories and poems which we are pleased to publish.

Edith Wharton died of a stroke in 1937 at the Domaine Le Pavillon Colombe, her 18th-century house on Rue de Montmorency in Saint-Brice-sous-Forêt.

Index of Contents

THE MUSE'S TRAGEDY

I

Danyers afterwards liked to fancy that he had recognized Mrs. Anerton at once; but that, of course, was absurd, since he had seen no portrait of her, she affected a strict anonymity, refusing even her photograph to the most privileged, and from Mrs. Memorall, whom he revered and cultivated as her friend, he had extracted but the one impressionist phrase: "Oh, well, she's like one of those old prints where the lines have the value of color."

He was almost certain, at all events, that he had been thinking of Mrs. Anerton as he sat over his breakfast in the empty hotel restaurant, and that, looking up on the approach of the lady who seated herself at the table near the window, he had said to himself, "That might be she."

Ever since his Harvard days—he was still young enough to think of them as immensely remote, Danyers had dreamed of Mrs. Anerton, the Silvia of Vincent Rendle's immortal sonnet-cycle, the Mrs. A. of the Life and Letters. Her name was enshrined in some of the noblest English verse of the nineteenth century, and of all past or future centuries, as Danyers, from the stand-point of a maturer judgment, still believed. The first reading of certain poems, of the Antinous, the Pia Tolomei, the Sonnets to Silvia, had been epochs in Danyers's growth, and the verse seemed to gain in mellowness, in amplitude, in meaning as one brought to its interpretation more experience of life, a finer emotional sense. Where, in his boyhood, he had felt only the perfect, the almost austere beauty of form, the subtle interplay of vowel-sounds, the rush and fulness of lyric emotion, he now thrilled to the close-packed significance of each line, the allusiveness of each word, his imagination lured hither and thither on fresh trails of thought, and perpetually spurred by the sense that, beyond what he had already discovered, more marvellous regions lay waiting to be explored. Danyers had written, at college, the prize essay on Rendle's poetry (it chanced to be the moment of the great man's death); he had fashioned the fugitive verse of his own storm-and-stress period on the forms which Rendle had first given to English metre; and when two years later the Life and Letters appeared, and the Silvia of the sonnets took substance as Mrs. A., he had included in his worship of Rendle the woman who had inspired not only such divine verse but such playful, tender, incomparable prose.

Danyers never forgot the day when Mrs. Memorall happened to mention that she knew Mrs. Anerton. He had known Mrs. Memorall for a year or more, and had somewhat contemptuously classified her as the kind of woman who runs cheap excursions to celebrities; when one afternoon she remarked, as she put a second lump of sugar in his tea:

"Is it right this time? You're almost as particular as Mary Anerton."

"Mary Anerton?"

"Yes, I never can remember how she likes her tea. Either it's lemon with sugar, or lemon without sugar, or cream without either, and whichever it is must be put into the cup before the tea is poured in; and if one hasn't remembered, one must begin all over again. I suppose it was Vincent Rendle's way of taking his tea and has become a sacred rite."

"Do you know Mrs. Anerton?" cried Danyers, disturbed by this careless familiarity with the habits of his divinity.

"'And did I once see Shelley plain?' Mercy, yes! She and I were at school together, she's an American, you know. We were at a pension near Tours for nearly a year; then she went back to New York, and I didn't see her again till after her marriage. She and Anerton spent a winter in Rome while my husband was attached to our Legation there, and she used to be with us a great deal." Mrs. Memorall smiled reminiscently. "It was the winter."

"The winter they first met?"

"Precisely, but unluckily I left Rome just before the meeting took place. Wasn't it too bad? I might have been in the Life and Letters. You know he mentions that stupid Madame Vodki, at whose house he first saw her."

"And did you see much of her after that?"

"Not during Rendle's life. You know she has lived in Europe almost entirely, and though I used to see her off and on when I went abroad, she was always so engrossed, so preoccupied, that one felt one wasn't wanted. The fact is, she cared only about his friends, she separated herself gradually from all her own people. Now, of course, it's different; she's desperately lonely; she's taken to writing to me now and then; and last year, when she heard I was going abroad, she asked me to meet her in Venice, and I spent a week with her there."

"And Rendle?"

Mrs. Memorall smiled and shook her head. "Oh, I never was allowed a peep at him; none of her old friends met him, except by accident. Ill-natured people say that was the reason she kept him so long. If one happened in while he was there, he was hustled into Anerton's study, and the husband mounted guard till the inopportune visitor had departed. Anerton, you know, was really much more ridiculous about it than his wife. Mary was too clever to lose her head, or at least to show she'd lost it, but Anerton couldn't conceal his pride in the conquest. I've seen Mary shiver when he spoke of Rendle as our poet. Rendle always had to have a certain seat at the dinner-table, away from the draught and not too near the fire, and a box of cigars that no one else was allowed to touch, and a writing-table of his own in Mary's sitting-room, and Anerton was always telling one of the great man's idiosyncrasies: how he never would cut the ends of his cigars, though Anerton himself had given him a gold cutter set with a star-sapphire, and how untidy his writing-table was, and how the house- maid had orders always to bring the waste-paper basket to her mistress before emptying it, lest some immortal verse should be thrown into the dust-bin."

"The Anertons never separated, did they?"

"Separated? Bless you, no. He never would have left Rendle! And besides, he was very fond of his wife."

"And she?"

"Oh, she saw he was the kind of man who was fated to make himself ridiculous, and she never interfered with his natural tendencies."

From Mrs. Memorall, Danyers further learned that Mrs. Anerton, whose husband had died some years before her poet, now divided her life between Rome, where she had a small apartment, and England, where she occasionally went to stay with those of her friends who had been Rendle's. She had been engaged, for some time after his death, in editing some juvenilia which he had bequeathed to her care; but that task being accomplished, she had been left without definite occupation, and Mrs. Memorall, on the occasion of their last meeting, had found her listless and out of spirits.

"She misses him too much, her life is too empty. I told her so, I told her she ought to marry."

"Oh!"

"Why not, pray? She's a young woman still, what many people would call young," Mrs. Memorall interjected, with a parenthetic glance at the mirror. "Why not accept the inevitable and begin over again? All the King's horses and all the King's men won't bring Rendle to life-and besides, she didn't marry him when she had the chance."

Danyers winced slightly at this rude fingering of his idol. Was it possible that Mrs. Memorall did not see what an anti-climax such a marriage would have been? Fancy Rendle "making an honest woman" of Silvia; for so society would have viewed it! How such a reparation would have vulgarized their past, it would have been like "restoring" a masterpiece; and how exquisite must have been the perceptions of the woman who, in defiance of appearances, and perhaps of her own secret inclination, chose to go down to posterity as Silvia rather than as Mrs. Vincent Rendle!

Mrs. Memorall, from this day forth, acquired an interest in Danyers's eyes. She was like a volume of unindexed and discursive memoirs, through which he patiently plodded in the hope of finding embedded amid layers of dusty twaddle some precious allusion to the subject of his thought. When, some months later, he brought out his first slim volume, in which the remodelled college essay on Rendle figured among a dozen, somewhat overstudied "appreciations," he offered a copy to Mrs. Memorall; who surprised him, the next time they met, with the announcement that she had sent the book to Mrs. Anerton.

Mrs. Anerton in due time wrote to thank her friend. Danyers was privileged to read the few lines in which, in terms that suggested the habit of "acknowledging" similar tributes, she spoke of the author's "feeling and insight," and was "so glad of the opportunity," etc. He went away disappointed, without clearly knowing what else he had expected.

The following spring, when he went abroad, Mrs. Memorall offered him letters to everybody, from the Archbishop of Canterbury to Louise Michel. She did not include Mrs. Anerton, however, and Danyers knew, from a previous conversation, that Silvia objected to people who "brought letters." He knew also that she travelled during the summer, and was unlikely to return to Rome before the term of his holiday should be reached, and the hope of meeting her was not included among his anticipations.

The lady whose entrance broke upon his solitary repast in the restaurant of the Hotel Villa d'Este had seated herself in such a way that her profile was detached against the window; and thus viewed, her domed forehead, small arched nose, and fastidious lip suggested a silhouette of Marie Antoinette. In the lady's dress and movements, in the very turn of her wrist as she poured out her coffee, Danyers thought he detected the same fastidiousness, the same air of tacitly excluding the obvious and unexceptional. Here was a woman who had been much bored and keenly interested. The waiter brought her a Secolo, and as she bent above it Danyers noticed that the hair rolled back from her forehead was turning gray; but her figure was straight and slender, and she had the invaluable gift of a girlish back.

The rush of Anglo-Saxon travel had not set toward the lakes, and with the exception of an Italian family or two, and a hump-backed youth with an abbe, Danyers and the lady had the marble halls of the Villa d'Este to themselves.

When he returned from his morning ramble among the hills he saw her sitting at one of the little tables at the edge of the lake. She was writing, and a heap of books and newspapers lay on the table at her side. That evening they met again in the garden. He had strolled out to smoke a last cigarette before dinner, and under the black vaulting of ilexes, near the steps leading down to the boat-landing, he found her leaning on the parapet above the lake. At the sound of his approach she turned and looked at him. She had thrown a black lace scarf over her head, and in this sombre setting her face seemed thin and unhappy. He remembered afterwards that her eyes, as they met his, expressed not so much sorrow as profound discontent.

To his surprise she stepped toward him with a detaining gesture.

"Mr. Lewis Danyers, I believe?"

He bowed.

"I am Mrs. Anerton. I saw your name on the visitors' list and wished to thank you for an essay on Mr. Rendle's poetry, or rather to tell you how much I appreciated it. The book was sent to me last winter by Mrs. Memorall."

She spoke in even melancholy tones, as though the habit of perfunctory utterance had robbed her voice of more spontaneous accents; but her smile was charming. They sat down on a stone bench under the ilexes, and she told him how much pleasure his essay had given her. She thought it the best in the book, she was sure he had put more of himself into it than into any other; was she not right in conjecturing that he had been very deeply influenced by Mr. Rendle's poetry? Pour comprendre il faut aimer, and it seemed to her that, in some ways, he had penetrated the poet's inner meaning more completely than any other critic. There were certain problems, of course, that he had left untouched; certain aspects of that many-sided mind that he had perhaps failed to seize,

"But then you are young," she concluded gently, "and one could not wish you, as yet, the experience that a fuller understanding would imply."

II

She stayed a month at Villa d'Este, and Danyers was with her daily. She showed an unaffected pleasure in his society; a pleasure so obviously founded on their common veneration of Rendle, that the young man could enjoy it without fear of fatuity. At first he was merely one more grain of frankincense on the altar of her insatiable divinity; but gradually a more personal note crept into their intercourse. If she still liked him only because he appreciated Rendle, she at least perceptibly distinguished him from the herd of Rendle's appreciators.

Her attitude toward the great man's memory struck Danyers as perfect. She neither proclaimed nor disavowed her identity. She was frankly Silvia to those who knew and cared; but there was no trace of the Egeria in her pose. She spoke often of Rendle's books, but seldom of himself; there was no posthumous conjugality, no use of the possessive tense, in her abounding reminiscences. Of the master's intellectual life, of his habits of thought and work, she never wearied of talking. She knew the history of each poem; by what scene or episode each image had been evoked; how many times the words in a certain line had been transposed; how long a certain adjective had been sought, and what had at last suggested it; she could even explain that one impenetrable line, the torment of critics, the joy of detractors, the last line of The Old Odysseus.

Danyers felt that in talking of these things she was no mere echo of Rendle's thought. If her identity had appeared to be merged in his it was because they thought alike, not because he had thought for her. Posterity is apt to regard the women whom poets have sung as chance pegs on which they hung their garlands; but Mrs. Anerton's mind was like some fertile garden wherein, inevitably, Rendle's imagination had rooted itself and flowered. Danyers began to see how many threads of his complex mental tissue the poet had owed to the blending of her temperament with his; in a certain sense Silvia had herself created the Sonnets to Silvia.

To be the custodian of Rendle's inner self, the door, as it were, to the sanctuary, had at first seemed to Danyers so comprehensive a privilege that he had the sense, as his friendship with Mrs. Anerton advanced, of forcing his way into a life already crowded. What room was there, among such towering memories, for so small an actuality as his? Quite suddenly, after this, he discovered that Mrs. Memorall knew better: his fortunate friend was bored as well as lonely.

"You have had more than any other woman!" he had exclaimed to her one day; and her smile flashed a derisive light on his blunder. Fool that he was, not to have seen that she had not had enough! That she was young still, do years count?—tender, human, a woman; that the living have need of the living.

After that, when they climbed the alleys of the hanging park, resting in one of the little ruined temples, or watching, through a ripple of foliage, the remote blue flash of the lake, they did not always talk of Rendle or of literature. She encouraged Danyers to speak of himself; to confide his ambitions to her; she asked him the questions which are the wise woman's substitute for advice.

"You must write," she said, administering the most exquisite flattery that human lips could give.

Of course he meant to write, why not to do something great in his turn? His best, at least; with the resolve, at the outset, that his best should be the best. Nothing less seemed possible with that mandate in his ears. How she had divined him; lifted and disentangled his groping ambitions; laid the awakening touch on his spirit with her creative Let there be light!

It was his last day with her, and he was feeling very hopeless and happy.

"You ought to write a book about him," she went on gently.

Danyers started; he was beginning to dislike Rendle's way of walking in unannounced.

"You ought to do it," she insisted. "A complete interpretation, a summing-up of his style, his purpose, his theory of life and art. No one else could do it as well."

He sat looking at her perplexedly. Suddenly—dared he guess?

"I couldn't do it without you," he faltered.

"I could help you—I would help you, of course."

They sat silent, both looking at the lake.

It was agreed, when they parted, that he should rejoin her six weeks later in Venice. There they were to talk about the book.

III

Lago d'Iseo, August 14th.

When I said good-by to you yesterday I promised to come back to Venice in a week: I was to give you your answer then. I was not honest in saying that; I didn't mean to go back to Venice or to see you again. I was running away from you—and I mean to keep on running! If you won't, I must. Somebody must save you from marrying a disappointed woman of—well, you say years don't count, and why should they, after all, since you are not to marry me?

That is what I dare not go back to say. You are not to marry me. We have had our month together in Venice (such a good month, was it not?) and now you are to go home and write a book—any book but the one we—didn't talk of!—and I am to stay here, attitudinizing among my memories like a sort of female Tithonus. The dreariness of this enforced immortality!

But you shall know the truth. I care for you, or at least for your love, enough to owe you that.

You thought it was because Vincent Rendle had loved me that there was so little hope for you. I had had what I wanted to the full; wasn't that what you said? It is just when a man begins to think he understands a woman that he may be sure he doesn't! It is because Vincent Rendle didn't love me that there is no hope for you. I never had what I wanted, and never, never, never will I stoop to wanting anything else.

Do you begin to understand? It was all a sham then, you say? No, it was all real as far as it went. You are young, you haven't learned, as you will later, the thousand imperceptible signs by which one gropes one's way through the labyrinth of human nature; but didn't it strike you, sometimes, that I never told you any foolish little anecdotes about him? His trick, for instance, of twirling a paper-knife round and round between his thumb and forefinger while he talked; his mania for saving the backs of notes; his greediness for wild strawberries, the little pungent Alpine ones; his childish delight in acrobats and jugglers; his way of always calling me you, dear you, every letter began, I never told you a word of all that, did I? Do you suppose I could have helped telling you, if he had loved me? These little things would have been mine, then, a part of my life, of our life, they would have slipped out in spite of me (it's only your unhappy woman who is always reticent and dignified). But there never was any "our life;" it was always "our lives" to the end....

If you knew what a relief it is to tell someone at last, you would bear with me, you would let me hurt you! I shall never be quite so lonely again, now that some one knows.

Let me begin at the beginning. When I first met Vincent Rendle I was not twenty-five. That was twenty years ago. From that time until his death, five years ago, we were fast friends. He gave me fifteen years, perhaps the best fifteen years, of his life. The world, as you know, thinks that his greatest poems were written during those years; I am supposed to have "inspired" them, and in a sense I did. From the first, the intellectual sympathy between us was almost complete; my mind must have been to him (I fancy) like some perfectly tuned instrument on which he was never tired of playing. Someone told me of his once saying of me that I "always understood;" it is the only praise I ever heard of his giving me. I don't even know if he thought me pretty, though I hardly think my appearance could have been disagreeable to him, for he hated to be with ugly people. At all events he fell into the way of spending more and more of his time with me. He liked our house; our ways suited him. He was nervous, irritable; people bored him and yet he disliked solitude. He took sanctuary with us. When we travelled he went with us; in the winter he took rooms near us in Rome. In England or on the continent he was always with us for a good part of the year. In small ways I was able to help him in his work; he grew dependent on me. When we were apart he wrote to me continually, he liked to have me share in all he was doing or thinking; he was impatient for my criticism of every new book that interested him; I was a part of his intellectual life. The pity of it was that I wanted to be something more. I was a young woman and I was in love with him, not because he was Vincent Rendle, but just because he was himself!

People began to talk, of course, I was Vincent Rendle's Mrs. Anerton; when the Sonnets to Silvia appeared, it was whispered that I was Silvia. Wherever he went, I was invited; people made up to me in the hope of getting to know him; when I was in London my doorbell never stopped ringing. Elderly peeresses, aspiring hostesses, love-sick girls and struggling authors overwhelmed me with their assiduities. I hugged my success, for I knew what it meant, they thought that Rendle was in love with me! Do you know, at times, they almost made me think so too? Oh, there was no phase of folly I didn't go through. You can't imagine the excuses a woman will invent for a man's not telling her that he loves her—pitiable arguments that she would see through at a glance if any other woman used them! But all the while, deep down, I knew he had never cared. I should have known it if he had made love to me every day of his life. I could never guess whether he knew what people said about us—he listened so little to what people said; and cared still less, when he heard. He was always quite honest and straightforward with me; he treated me as one man treats another; and yet at times I felt he must see that with me it was different. If he did see, he made no sign. Perhaps he never noticed, I am sure he never meant to be cruel. He had never made love to me; it was no fault of his if I wanted more than he could give me. The Sonnets to Silvia, you say? But what are they? A cosmic philosophy, not a love-poem; addressed to Woman, not to a woman!

But then, the letters? Ah, the letters! Well, I'll make a clean breast of it. You have noticed the breaks in the letters here and there, just as they seem to be on the point of growing a little—warmer? The critics, you may remember, praised the editor for his commendable delicacy and good taste (so rare in these days!) in omitting from the correspondence all personal allusions, all those details intimes which should be kept sacred from the public gaze. They referred, of course, to the asterisks in the letters to Mrs. A. Those letters I myself prepared for publication; that is to say, I copied them out for the editor, and every now and then I put in a line of asterisks to make it appear that something had been left out. You understand? The asterisks were a sham, there was nothing to leave out.

No one but a woman could understand what I went through during those years, the moments of revolt, when I felt I must break away from it all, fling the truth in his face and never see him again; the inevitable reaction, when not to see him seemed the one unendurable thing, and I trembled lest a look or word of mine should disturb the poise of our friendship; the silly days when I hugged the delusion that he must love me, since everybody thought he did; the long periods of numbness, when I didn't seem to care whether he loved me or not. Between these wretched days came others when our intellectual accord was so perfect that I forgot everything else in the joy of feeling myself lifted up on the wings of his thought. Sometimes, then, the heavens seemed to be opened....

All this time he was so dear a friend! He had the genius of friendship, and he spent it all on me. Yes, you were right when you said that I have had more than any other woman. Il faut de l'adresse pour aimer, Pascal says; and I was so quiet, so cheerful, so frankly affectionate with him, that in all those years I am almost sure I never bored him. Could I have hoped as much if he had loved me?

You mustn't think of him, though, as having been tied to my skirts. He came and went as he pleased, and so did his fancies. There was a girl once (I am telling you everything), a lovely being who called his poetry "deep" and gave him Lucile on his birthday. He followed her to Switzerland one summer, and all the time that he was dangling after her (a little too conspicuously, I always thought, for a Great Man), he was writing to me about his theory of vowel-combinations, or was it his experiments in English hexameter? The letters were dated from the very places where I knew they went and sat by waterfalls together and he thought out adjectives for her hair. He talked to me about it quite frankly afterwards. She was perfectly beautiful and it had been a pure delight to watch her; but she would talk, and her mind, he said, was "all elbows." And yet, the next year, when her marriage was announced, he went away alone, quite suddenly ... and it was just afterwards that he published Love's Viaticum. Men are queer!

After my husband died, I am putting things crudely, you see, I had a return of hope. It was because he loved me, I argued, that he had never spoken; because he had always hoped some day to make me his wife; because he wanted to spare me the "reproach." Rubbish! I knew well enough, in my heart of hearts, that my one chance lay in the force of habit. He had grown used to me; he was no longer young; he dreaded new people and new ways; il avait pris son pli. Would it not be easier to marry me?

I don't believe he ever thought of it. He wrote me what people call "a beautiful letter;" he was kind; considerate, decently commiserating; then, after a few weeks, he slipped into his old way of coming in every afternoon, and our interminable talks began again just where they had left off. I heard later that people thought I had shown "such good taste" in not marrying him.

So we jogged on for five years longer. Perhaps they were the best years, for I had given up hoping. Then he died.

After his death, this is curious, there came to me a kind of mirage of love. All the books and articles written about him, all the reviews of the "Life," were full of discreet allusions to Silvia. I became again the Mrs. Anerton of the glorious days. Sentimental girls and dear lads like you turned pink when somebody whispered, "that was Silvia you were talking to." Idiots begged for my autograph, publishers urged me to write my reminiscences of him, critics consulted me about the reading of doubtful lines. And I knew that, to all these people, I was the woman Vincent Rendle had loved.

After a while that fire went out too and I was left alone with my past. Alone, quite alone; for he had never really been with me. The intellectual union counted for nothing now. It had been soul to soul, but never hand in hand, and there were no little things to remember him by.

Then there set in a kind of Arctic winter. I crawled into myself as into a snow-hut. I hated my solitude and yet dreaded anyone who disturbed it. That phase, of course, passed like the others. I took up life again, and began to read the papers and consider the cut of my gowns. But there was one question that I could not be rid of, that haunted me night and day. Why had he never loved me? Why had I been so much to him, and no more? Was I so ugly, so essentially unlovable, that though a man might cherish me as his mind's comrade, he could not care for me as a woman? I can't tell you how that question tortured me. It became an obsession.

My poor friend, do you begin to see? I had to find out what some other man thought of me. Don't be too hard on me! Listen first—consider. When I first met Vincent Rendle I was a young woman, who had married early and led the quietest kind of life; I had had no "experiences." From the hour of our first meeting to the day of his death I never looked at any other man, and never noticed whether any other man looked at me. When he died, five years ago, I knew the extent of my powers no more than a baby. Was it too late to find out? Should I never know why?

Forgive me, forgive me. You are so young; it will be an episode, a mere "document," to you so soon! And, besides, it wasn't as deliberate, as cold-blooded as these disjointed lines have made it appear. I didn't plan it, like a woman in a book. Life is so much more complex than any rendering of it can be. I liked you from the first—I was drawn to you (you must have seen that) I wanted you to like me; it was not a mere psychological experiment. And yet in a sense it was that, too, I must be honest. I had to have an answer to that question; it was a ghost that had to be laid.

At first I was afraid, oh, so much afraid, that you cared for me only because I was Silvia, that you loved me because you thought Rendle had loved me. I began to think there was no escaping my destiny.

How happy I was when I discovered that you were growing jealous of my past; that you actually hated Rendle! My heart beat like a girl's when you told me you meant to follow me to Venice.

After our parting at Villa d'Este my old doubts reasserted themselves. What did I know of your feeling for me, after all? Were you capable of analyzing it yourself? Was it not likely to be two-thirds vanity and curiosity, and one-third literary sentimentality? You might easily fancy that you cared for Mary Anerton when you were really in love with Silvia—the heart is such a hypocrite! Or you might be more calculating than I had supposed. Perhaps it was you who had been flattering my vanity in the hope (the pardonable hope!) of turning me, after a decent interval, into a pretty little essay with a margin.

When you arrived in Venice and we met again, do you remember the music on the lagoon, that evening, from my balcony?—I was so afraid you would begin to talk about the book, the book, you remember, was your ostensible reason for coming. You never spoke of it, and I soon saw your one fear was I might do so, might remind you of your object in being with me. Then I knew you cared for me! yes, at that moment really cared! We never mentioned the book once, did we, during that month in Venice?

I have read my letter over; and now I wish that I had said this to you instead of writing it. I could have felt my way then, watching your face and seeing if you understood. But, no, I could not go back to Venice; and I could not tell you (though I tried) while we were there together. I couldn't spoil that month, my one month. It was so good, for once in my life, to get away from literature....

You will be angry with me at first, but, alas! not for long. What I have done would have been cruel if I had been a younger woman; as it is, the experiment will hurt no one but myself. And it will hurt me horribly (as much as, in your first anger, you may perhaps wish), because it has shown me, for the first time, all that I have missed....

A JOURNEY

As she lay in her berth, staring at the shadows overhead, the rush of the wheels was in her brain, driving her deeper and deeper into circles of wakeful lucidity. The sleeping-car had sunk into its night-silence. Through the wet window-pane she watched the sudden lights, the long stretches of hurrying blackness. Now and then she turned her head and looked through the opening in the hangings at her husband's curtains across the aisle....

She wondered restlessly if he wanted anything and if she could hear him if he called. His voice had grown very weak within the last months and it irritated him when she did not hear. This irritability, this increasing childish petulance seemed to give expression to their imperceptible estrangement. Like two faces looking at one another through a sheet of glass they were close together, almost touching, but they could not hear or feel each other: the conductivity between them was broken. She, at least, had this sense of separation, and she fancied sometimes that she saw it reflected in the look with which he supplemented his failing words. Doubtless the fault was hers. She was too impenetrably healthy to be touched by the irrelevancies of disease. Her self-reproachful tenderness was tinged with the sense of his irrationality: she had a vague feeling that there was a purpose in his helpless tyrannies. The suddenness of the change had found her so unprepared. A year ago their pulses had beat to one robust measure; both had the same prodigal confidence in an exhaustless future. Now their energies no longer kept step: hers still bounded ahead of life, preempting unclaimed regions of hope and activity, while his lagged behind, vainly struggling to overtake her.

When they married, she had such arrears of living to make up: her days had been as bare as the whitewashed school-room where she forced innutritious facts upon reluctant children. His coming had broken in on the slumber of circumstance, widening the present till it became the encloser of remotest chances. But imperceptibly the horizon narrowed. Life had a grudge against her: she was never to be allowed to spread her wings.

At first the doctors had said that six weeks of mild air would set him right; but when he came back this assurance was explained as having of course included a winter in a dry climate. They gave up their pretty house, storing the wedding presents and new furniture, and went to Colorado. She had hated it there from the first. Nobody knew her or cared about her; there was no one to wonder at the good match she had made, or to envy her the new dresses and the visiting-cards which were still a surprise to her. And he kept growing worse. She felt herself beset with difficulties too evasive to be fought by so direct a temperament. She still loved him, of course; but he was gradually, undefinably ceasing to be himself. The man she had married had been strong, active, gently masterful: the male whose pleasure it is to clear a way through the material obstructions of life; but now it was she who was the protector, he who must be shielded from importunities and given his drops or his beef-juice though the skies were falling. The routine of the sick-room bewildered her; this punctual administering of medicine seemed as idle as some uncomprehended religious mummery.

There were moments, indeed, when warm gushes of pity swept away her instinctive resentment of his condition, when she still found his old self in his eyes as they groped for each other through the dense medium of his weakness. But these moments had grown rare. Sometimes he frightened her: his sunken expressionless face seemed that of a stranger; his voice was weak and hoarse; his thin-lipped smile a mere muscular contraction. Her hand avoided his damp soft skin, which had lost the familiar roughness of health: she caught herself furtively watching him as she might have watched a strange animal. It frightened her to feel that this was the man she loved; there were hours when to tell him what she suffered seemed the one escape from her fears. But in general she judged herself more leniently, reflecting that she had perhaps been too long alone with him, and that she would feel differently when they were at home again, surrounded by her robust and buoyant family. How she had rejoiced when the doctors at last gave their consent to his going home! She knew, of course, what the decision meant; they both knew. It meant that he was to die; but they dressed the truth in hopeful euphuisms, and at times, in the joy of preparation, she really forgot the purpose of their journey, and slipped into an eager allusion to next year's plans.

At last the day of leaving came. She had a dreadful fear that they would never get away; that somehow at the last moment he would fail her; that the doctors held one of their accustomed treacheries in reserve; but nothing happened. They drove to the station, he was installed in a seat with a rug over his knees and a cushion at his back, and she hung out of the window waving unregretful farewells to the acquaintances she had really never liked till then.

The first twenty-four hours had passed off well. He revived a little and it amused him to look out of the window and to observe the humours of the car. The second day he began to grow weary and to chafe under the dispassionate stare of the freckled child with the lump of chewing-gum. She had to explain to the child's mother that her husband was too ill to be disturbed: a statement received by that lady with a resentment visibly supported by the maternal sentiment of the whole car....

That night he slept badly and the next morning his temperature frightened her: she was sure he was growing worse. The day passed slowly, punctuated by the small irritations of travel. Watching his tired face, she traced in its contractions every rattle and jolt of the tram, till her own body vibrated with sympathetic fatigue. She felt the others observing him too, and hovered restlessly between him and the line of interrogative eyes. The freckled child hung about him like a fly; offers of candy and picture- books failed to dislodge her: she twisted one leg around the other and watched him imperturbably. The porter, as he passed, lingered with vague proffers of help, probably inspired by philanthropic passengers swelling with the sense that "something ought to be done;" and one nervous man in a skull-cap was audibly concerned as to the possible effect on his wife's health.

The hours dragged on in a dreary inoccupation. Towards dusk she sat down beside him and he laid his hand on hers. The touch startled her. He seemed to be calling her from far off. She looked at him helplessly and his smile went through her like a physical pang.

"Are you very tired?" she asked.

"No, not very."

"We'll be there soon now."

"Yes, very soon."

"This time to-morrow—"

He nodded and they sat silent. When she had put him to bed and crawled into her own berth she tried to cheer herself with the thought that in less than twenty-four hours they would be in New York. Her people would all be at the station to meet her—she pictured their round unanxious faces pressing through the crowd. She only hoped they would not tell him too loudly that he was looking splendidly and would be all right in no time: the subtler sympathies developed by long contact with suffering were making her aware of a certain coarseness of texture in the family sensibilities.

Suddenly she thought she heard him call. She parted the curtains and listened. No, it was only a man snoring at the other end of the car. His snores had a greasy sound, as though they passed through tallow. She lay down and tried to sleep... Had she not heard him move? She started up trembling... The silence frightened her more than any sound. He might not be able to make her hear, he might be calling her now... What made her think of such things? It was merely the familiar tendency of an over-tired mind to fasten itself on the most intolerable chance within the range of its forebodings.... Putting her head out, she listened; but she could not distinguish his breathing from that of the other pairs of lungs about her. She longed to get up and look at him, but she knew the impulse was a mere vent for her restlessness, and the fear of disturbing him restrained her.... The regular movement of his curtain reassured her, she knew not why; she remembered that he had wished her a cheerful good-night; and the sheer inability to endure her fears a moment longer made her put them from her with an effort of her whole sound tired body. She turned on her side and slept.

She sat up stiffly, staring out at the dawn. The train was rushing through a region of bare hillocks huddled against a lifeless sky. It looked like the first day of creation. The air of the car was close, and she pushed up her window to let in the keen wind. Then she looked at her watch: it was seven o'clock, and soon the people about her would be stirring. She slipped into her clothes, smoothed her dishevelled hair and crept to the dressing-room. When she had washed her face and adjusted her dress she felt more hopeful. It was always a struggle for her not to be cheerful in the morning. Her cheeks burned deliciously under the coarse towel and the wet hair about her temples broke into strong upward tendrils. Every inch of her was full of life and elasticity. And in ten hours they would be at home!

She stepped to her husband's berth: it was time for him to take his early glass of milk. The window-shade was down, and in the dusk of the curtained enclosure she could just see that he lay sideways, with his face away from her. She leaned over him and drew up the shade. As she did so she touched one of his hands. It felt cold....

She bent closer, laying her hand on his arm and calling him by name. He did not move. She spoke again more loudly; she grasped his shoulder and gently shook it. He lay motionless. She caught hold of his hand again: it slipped from her limply, like a dead thing. A dead thing? ... Her breath caught. She must see his face. She leaned forward, and hurriedly, shrinkingly, with a sickening reluctance of the flesh, laid her hands on his shoulders and turned him over. His head fell back; his face looked small and smooth; he gazed at her with steady eyes.

She remained motionless for a long time, holding him thus; and they looked at each other. Suddenly she shrank back: the longing to scream, to call out, to fly from him, had almost overpowered her. But a strong hand arrested her. Good God! If it were known that he was dead they would be put off the train at the next station—

In a terrifying flash of remembrance there arose before her a scene she had once witnessed in travelling, when a husband and wife, whose child had died in the train, had been thrust out at some chance station. She saw them standing on the platform with the child's body between them; she had never forgotten the dazed look with which they followed the receding train. And this was what would happen to her. Within the next hour she might find herself on the platform of some strange station, alone with her husband's body.... Anything but that! It was too horrible—She quivered like a creature at bay.

As she cowered there, she felt the train moving more slowly. It was coming then, they were approaching a station! She saw again the husband and wife standing on the lonely platform; and with a violent gesture she drew down the shade to hide her husband's face.

Feeling dizzy, she sank down on the edge of the berth, keeping away from his outstretched body, and pulling the curtains close, so that he and she were shut into a kind of sepulchral twilight. She tried to think. At all costs she must conceal the fact that he was dead. But how? Her mind refused to act: she could not plan, combine. She could think of no way but to sit there, clutching the curtains, all day long....

She heard the porter making up her bed; people were beginning to move about the car; the dressing-room door was being opened and shut. She tried to rouse herself. At length with a supreme effort she rose to her feet, stepping into the aisle of the car and drawing the curtains tight behind her. She noticed that they still parted slightly with the motion of the car, and finding a pin in her dress she fastened them together. Now she was safe. She looked round and saw the porter. She fancied he was watching her.

"Ain't he awake yet?" he enquired.

"No," she faltered.

"I got his milk all ready when he wants it. You know you told me to have it for him by seven."

She nodded silently and crept into her seat.

At half-past eight the train reached Buffalo. By this time the other passengers were dressed and the berths had been folded back for the day. The porter, moving to and fro under his burden of sheets and pillows, glanced at her as he passed. At length he said: "Ain't he going to get up? You know we're ordered to make up the berths as early as we can."

She turned cold with fear. They were just entering the station.

"Oh, not yet," she stammered. "Not till he's had his milk. Won't you get it, please?"

"All right. Soon as we start again."

When the train moved on he reappeared with the milk. She took it from him and sat vaguely looking at it: her brain moved slowly from one idea to another, as though they were stepping-stones set far apart across a whirling flood. At length she became aware that the porter still hovered expectantly.

"Will I give it to him?" he suggested.

"Oh, no," she cried, rising. "He—he's asleep yet, I think—"

She waited till the porter had passed on; then she unpinned the curtains and slipped behind them. In the semi-obscurity her husband's face stared up at her like a marble mask with agate eyes. The eyes were dreadful. She put out her hand and drew down the lids. Then she remembered the glass of milk in her other hand: what was she to do with it? She thought of raising the window and throwing it out; but to do so she would have to lean across his body and bring her face close to his. She decided to drink the milk.

She returned to her seat with the empty glass and after a while the porter came back to get it.

"When'll I fold up his bed?" he asked.

"Oh, not now, not yet; he's ill, he's very ill. Can't you let him stay as he is? The doctor wants him to lie down as much as possible."

He scratched his head. "Well, if he's really sick—"

He took the empty glass and walked away, explaining to the passengers that the party behind the curtains was too sick to get up just yet.

She found herself the centre of sympathetic eyes. A motherly woman with an intimate smile sat down beside her.

"I'm real sorry to hear your husband's sick. I've had a remarkable amount of sickness in my family and maybe I could assist you. Can I take a look at him?"

"Oh, no, no, please! He mustn't be disturbed."

The lady accepted the rebuff indulgently.

"Well, it's just as you say, of course, but you don't look to me as if you'd had much experience in sickness and I'd have been glad to assist you. What do you generally do when your husband's taken this way?"

"I—I let him sleep."

"Too much sleep ain't any too healthful either. Don't you give him any medicine?"

"Y—yes."

"Don't you wake him to take it?"

"Yes."

"When does he take the next dose?"

"Not for—two hours—"

The lady looked disappointed. "Well, if I was you I'd try giving it oftener. That's what I do with my folks."

After that many faces seemed to press upon her. The passengers were on their way to the dining-car, and she was conscious that as they passed down the aisle they glanced curiously at the closed curtains. One lantern- jawed man with prominent eyes stood still and tried to shoot his projecting glance through the division between the folds. The freckled child, returning from breakfast, waylaid the passers with a buttery clutch, saying in a loud whisper, "He's sick;" and once the conductor came by, asking for tickets. She shrank into her corner and looked out of the window at the flying trees and houses, meaningless hieroglyphs of an endlessly unrolled papyrus.

Now and then the train stopped, and the newcomers on entering the car stared in turn at the closed curtains. More and more people seemed to pass—their faces began to blend fantastically with the images surging in her brain....

Later in the day a fat man detached himself from the mist of faces. He had a creased stomach and soft pale lips. As he pressed himself into the seat facing her she noticed that he was dressed in black broadcloth, with a soiled white tie.

"Husband's pretty bad this morning, is he?"

"Yes."

"Dear, dear! Now that's terribly distressing, ain't it?" An apostolic smile revealed his gold-filled teeth.

"Of course you know there's no sech thing as sickness. Ain't that a lovely thought? Death itself is but a deloosion of our grosser senses. On'y lay yourself open to the influx of the sperrit, submit yourself passively to the action of the divine force, and disease and dissolution will cease to exist for you. If you could indooce your husband to read this little pamphlet—"

The faces about her again grew indistinct. She had a vague recollection of hearing the motherly lady and the parent of the freckled child ardently disputing the relative advantages of trying several medicines at once, or of taking each in turn; the motherly lady maintaining that the competitive system saved time; the other objecting that you couldn't tell which remedy had effected the cure; their voices went on and on, like bell-buoys droning through a fog.... The porter came up now and then with questions that she did not understand, but that somehow she must have answered since he went away again without repeating them; every two hours the motherly lady reminded her that her husband ought to have his drops; people left the car and others replaced them...

Her head was spinning and she tried to steady herself by clutching at her thoughts as they swept by, but they slipped away from her like bushes on the side of a sheer precipice down which she seemed to be falling. Suddenly her mind grew clear again and she found herself vividly picturing what would happen when the train reached New York. She shuddered as it occurred to her that he would be quite cold and that someone might perceive he had been dead since morning.

She thought hurriedly:—"If they see I am not surprised they will suspect something. They will ask questions, and if I tell them the truth they won't believe me, no one would believe me! It will be terrible"—and she kept repeating to herself:—"I must pretend I don't know. I must pretend I don't know. When they open the curtains I must go up to him quite naturally—and then I must scream." ... She had an idea that the scream would be very hard to do.

Gradually new thoughts crowded upon her, vivid and urgent: she tried to separate and restrain them, but they beset her clamorously, like her school-children at the end of a hot day, when she was too tired to silence them. Her head grew confused, and she felt a sick fear of forgetting her part, of betraying herself by some unguarded word or look.

"I must pretend I don't know," she went on murmuring. The words had lost their significance, but she repeated them mechanically, as though they had been a magic formula, until suddenly she heard herself saying: "I can't remember, I can't remember!"

Her voice sounded very loud, and she looked about her in terror; but no one seemed to notice that she had spoken.

As she glanced down the car her eye caught the curtains of her husband's berth, and she began to examine the monotonous arabesques woven through their heavy folds. The pattern was intricate and difficult to trace; she gazed fixedly at the curtains and as she did so the thick stuff grew transparent and through it she saw her husband's face, his dead face. She struggled to avert her look, but her eyes refused to move and her head seemed to be held in a vice. At last, with an effort that left her weak and shaking, she turned away; but it was of no use; close in front of her, small and smooth, was her husband's face. It seemed to be suspended in the air between her and the false braids of the woman who sat in front of her. With an uncontrollable gesture she stretched out her hand to push the face away, and suddenly she felt the touch of his smooth skin. She repressed a cry and half started from her seat. The woman with the false braids looked around, and feeling that she must justify her movement in some way she rose and lifted her travelling-bag from the opposite seat. She unlocked the bag and looked into it; but the first object her hand met was a small flask of her husband's, thrust there at the last moment, in the haste of departure. She locked the bag and closed her eyes ... his face was there again, hanging between her eye-balls and lids like a waxen mask against a red curtain....

She roused herself with a shiver. Had she fainted or slept? Hours seemed to have elapsed; but it was still broad day, and the people about her were sitting in the same attitudes as before.

A sudden sense of hunger made her aware that she had eaten nothing since morning. The thought of food filled her with disgust, but she dreaded a return of faintness, and remembering that she had some biscuits in her bag she took one out and ate it. The dry crumbs choked her, and she hastily swallowed a little brandy from her husband's flask. The burning sensation in her throat acted as a counter-irritant, momentarily relieving the dull ache of her nerves. Then she felt a gently-stealing warmth, as though a soft air fanned her, and the swarming fears relaxed their clutch, receding through the stillness that enclosed her, a stillness soothing as the spacious quietude of a summer day. She slept.

Through her sleep she felt the impetuous rush of the train. It seemed to be life itself that was sweeping her on with headlong inexorable force—sweeping her into darkness and terror, and the awe of unknown days. Now all at once everything was still, not a sound, not a pulsation... She was dead in her turn, and lay beside him with smooth upstaring face. How quiet it was!—and yet she heard feet coming, the feet of the men who were to carry them away... She could feel too, she felt a sudden prolonged vibration, a series of hard shocks, and then another plunge into darkness: the darkness of death this time, a black whirlwind on which they were both spinning like leaves, in wild uncoiling spirals, with millions and millions of the dead....

She sprang up in terror. Her sleep must have lasted a long time, for the winter day had paled and the lights had been lit. The car was in confusion, and as she regained her self-possession she saw that the passengers were gathering up their wraps and bags. The woman with the false braids had brought from the dressing-room a sickly ivy-plant in a bottle, and the Christian Scientist was reversing his cuffs. The porter passed down the aisle with his impartial brush. An impersonal figure with a gold-banded cap asked for her husband's ticket. A voice shouted "Baig- gage express!" and she heard the clicking of metal as the passengers handed over their checks.

Presently her window was blocked by an expanse of sooty wall, and the train passed into the Harlem tunnel. The journey was over; in a few minutes she would see her family pushing their joyous way through the throng at the station. Her heart dilated. The worst terror was past....

"We'd better get him up now, hadn't we?" asked the porter, touching her arm.

He had her husband's hat in his hand and was meditatively revolving it under his brush.

She looked at the hat and tried to speak; but suddenly the car grew dark. She flung up her arms, struggling to catch at something, and fell face downward, striking her head against the dead man's berth.

THE PELICAN

She was very pretty when I first knew her, with the sweet straight nose and short upper lip of the cameo-brooch divinity, humanized by a dimple that flowered in her cheek whenever anything was said possessing the outward attributes of humor without its intrinsic quality. For the dear lady was providentially deficient in humor: the least hint of the real thing clouded her lovely eye like the hovering shadow of an algebraic problem.

I don't think nature had meant her to be "intellectual;" but what can a poor thing do, whose husband has died of drink when her baby is hardly six months old, and who finds her coral necklace and her grandfather's edition of the British Dramatists inadequate to the demands of the creditors?

Her mother, the celebrated Irene Astarte Pratt, had written a poem in blank verse on "The Fall of Man;" one of her aunts was dean of a girls' college; another had translated Euripides, with such a family, the poor child's fate was sealed in advance. The only way of paying her husband's debts and keeping the baby clothed was to be intellectual; and, after some hesitation as to the form her mental activity was to take, it was unanimously decided that she was to give lectures.

They began by being drawing-room lectures. The first time I saw her she was standing by the piano, against a flippant background of Dresden china and photographs, telling a roomful of women preoccupied with their spring bonnets all she thought she knew about Greek art. The ladies assembled to hear her had given me to understand that she was "doing it for the baby," and this fact, together with the shortness of her upper lip and the bewildering co-operation of her dimple, disposed me to listen leniently to her dissertation. Happily, at that time Greek art was still, if I may use the phrase, easily handled: it was as simple as walking down a museum- gallery lined with pleasant familiar Venuses and Apollos. All the later complications, the archaic and archaistic conundrums; the influences of Assyria and Asia Minor; the conflicting attributions and the wrangles of the erudite, still slumbered in the bosom of the future "scientific critic." Greek art in those days began with Phidias and ended with the Apollo Belvedere; and a child could travel from one to the other without danger of losing his way.

Mrs. Amyot had two fatal gifts: a capacious but inaccurate memory, and an extraordinary fluency of speech. There was nothing she did not remember—wrongly; but her halting facts were swathed in so many layers of rhetoric that their infirmities were imperceptible to her friendly critics. Besides, she had been taught Greek by the aunt who had translated Euripides; and the mere sound of the [Greek: ais] and [Greek: ois] that she now and then not unskilfully let slip (correcting herself, of course, with a start, and indulgently mistranslating the phrase), struck awe to the hearts of ladies whose only "accomplishment" was French—if you didn't speak too quickly.

I had then but a momentary glimpse of Mrs. Amyot, but a few months later I came upon her again in the New England university town where the celebrated Irene Astarte Pratt lived on the summit of a local Parnassus, with lesser muses and college professors respectfully grouped on the lower ledges of the sacred declivity. Mrs. Amyot, who, after her husband's death, had returned to the maternal roof (even during her father's lifetime the roof had been distinctively maternal), Mrs. Amyot, thanks to her upper lip, her dimple and her Greek, was already esconced in a snug hollow of the Parnassian slope.

After the lecture was over it happened that I walked home with Mrs. Amyot. From the incensed glances of two or three learned gentlemen who were hovering on the door-step when we emerged, I inferred that Mrs. Amyot, at that period, did not often walk home alone; but I doubt whether any of my discomfited rivals, whatever his claims to favor, was ever treated to so ravishing a mixture of shyness and self-abandonment, of sham erudition and real teeth and hair, as it was my privilege to enjoy. Even at the opening of her public career Mrs. Amyot had a tender eye for strangers, as possible links with successive centres of culture to which in due course the torch of Greek art might be handed on.

She began by telling me that she had never been so frightened in her life. She knew, of course, how dreadfully learned I was, and when, just as she was going to begin, her hostess had whispered to her that I was in the room, she had felt ready to sink through the floor. Then (with a flying dimple) she had remembered Emerson's line—wasn't it Emerson's?—that beauty is its own excuse for seeing, and that had made her feel a little more confident, since she was sure that no one saw beauty more vividly than she, as a child she used to sit for hours gazing at an Etruscan vase on the bookcase in the library, while her sisters played with their dolls, and if seeing beauty was the only excuse one needed for talking about it, why, she was sure I would make allowances and not be too critical and sarcastic, especially if, as she thought probable, I had heard of her having lost her poor husband, and how she had to do it for the baby.

Being abundantly assured of my sympathy on these points, she went on to say that she had always wanted so much to consult me about her lectures. Of course, one subject wasn't enough (this view of the limitations of Greek art as a "subject" gave me a startling idea of the rate at which a successful lecturer might exhaust the universe); she must find others; she had not ventured on any as yet, but she had thought of Tennyson—didn't I love Tennyson? She worshipped him so that she was sure she could help others to understand him; or what did I think of a "course" on Raphael or Michelangelo, or on the heroines of Shakespeare? There were some fine steel-engravings of Raphael's Madonnas and of the Sistine ceiling in her mother's library, and she had seen Miss Cushman in several Shakespearian roles, so that on these subjects also she felt qualified to speak with authority.

When we reached her mother's door she begged me to come in and talk the matter over; she wanted me to see the baby, she felt as though I should understand her better if I saw the baby, and the dimple flashed through a tear.

The fear of encountering the author of "The Fall of Man," combined with the opportune recollection of a dinner engagement, made me evade this appeal with the promise of returning on the morrow. On the morrow, I left too early to redeem my promise; and for several years afterwards I saw no more of Mrs. Amyot.

My calling at that time took me at irregular intervals from one to another of our larger cities, and as Mrs. Amyot was also peripatetic it was inevitable that sooner or later we should cross each other's path. It was therefore without surprise that, one snowy afternoon in Boston, I learned from the lady with whom I chanced to be lunching that, as soon as the meal was over, I was to be taken to hear Mrs. Amyot lecture.

"On Greek art?" I suggested.

"Oh, you've heard her then? No, this is one of the series called 'Homes and Haunts of the Poets.' Last week we had Wordsworth and the Lake Poets, to-day we are to have Goethe and Weimar. She is a wonderful creature, all the women of her family are geniuses. You know, of course, that her mother was Irene Astarte Pratt, who wrote a poem on 'The Fall of Man'; N.P. Willis called her the female Milton of America. One of Mrs. Amyot's aunts has translated Eurip—"

"And is she as pretty as ever?" I irrelevantly interposed.

My hostess looked shocked. "She is excessively modest and retiring. She says it is actual suffering for her to speak in public. You know she only does it for the baby."

Punctually at the hour appointed, we took our seats in a lecture-hall full of strenuous females in ulsters. Mrs. Amyot was evidently a favorite with these austere sisters, for every corner was crowded, and as we entered a pale usher with an educated mispronunciation was setting forth to several dejected applicants the impossibility of supplying them with seats.

Our own were happily so near the front that when the curtains at the back of the platform parted, and Mrs. Amyot appeared, I was at once able to establish a comparison between the lady placidly dimpling to the applause of her public and the shrinking drawing-room orator of my earlier recollections.

Mrs. Amyot was as pretty as ever, and there was the same curious discrepancy between the freshness of her aspect and the stateness of her theme, but something was gone of the blushing unsteadiness with which she had fired her first random shots at Greek art. It was not that the shots were less uncertain, but that she now had an air of assuming that, for her purpose, the bull's-eye was everywhere, so that there was no need to be flustered in taking aim. This assurance had so facilitated the flow of her eloquence that she seemed to be performing a trick analogous to that of the conjuror who pulls hundreds of yards of white paper out of his mouth. From a large assortment of stock adjectives she chose, with unerring deftness and rapidity, the one that taste and discrimination would most surely have rejected, fitting out her subject with a whole wardrobe of slop-shop epithets irrelevant in cut and size. To the invaluable knack of not disturbing the association of ideas in her audience, she added the gift of what may be called a confidential manner, so that her fluent generalizations about Goethe and his place in literature (the lecture was, of course, manufactured out of Lewes's book) had the flavor of personal experience, of views sympathetically exchanged with her audience on the best way of knitting children's socks, or of putting up preserves for the winter. It was, I am sure, to this personal accent, the moral equivalent of her dimple, that Mrs. Amyot owed her prodigious, her irrational success. It was her art of transposing second-hand ideas into first-hand emotions that so endeared her to her feminine listeners.

To any one not in search of "documents" Mrs. Amyot's success was hardly of a kind to make her more interesting, and my curiosity flagged with the growing conviction that the "suffering" entailed on her by public speaking was at most a retrospective pang. I was sure that she had reached the point of measuring and enjoying her effects, of deliberately manipulating her public; and there must indeed have been a certain exhilaration in attaining results so considerable by means involving so little conscious effort. Mrs. Amyot's art was simply an extension of coquetry: she flirted with her audience.

In this mood of enlightened skepticism I responded but languidly to my hostess's suggestion that I should go with her that evening to see Mrs. Amyot. The aunt who had translated Euripides was at home on Saturday evenings, and one met "thoughtful" people there, my hostess explained: it was one of the intellectual centres of Boston. My mood remained distinctly resentful of any connection between Mrs. Amyot and intellectuality, and I declined to go; but the next day I met Mrs. Amyot in the street.

She stopped me reproachfully. She had heard I was in Boston; why had I not come last night? She had been told that I was at her lecture, and it had frightened her, yes, really, almost as much as years ago in Hillbridge. She never could get over that stupid shyness, and the whole business was as distasteful to her as ever; but what could she do? There was the baby—he was a big boy now, and boys were so expensive! But did I really think she had improved the least little bit? And why wouldn't I come home with her now, and see the boy, and tell her frankly what I had thought of the lecture? She had plenty of flattery, people were so kind, and everyone knew that she did it for the baby, but what she felt the need of was criticism, severe, discriminating criticism like mine, oh, she knew that I was dreadfully discriminating!

I went home with her and saw the boy. In the early heat of her Tennyson- worship Mrs. Amyot had christened him Lancelot, and he looked it. Perhaps, however, it was his black velvet dress and the exasperating length of his yellow curls, together with the fact of his having been taught to recite Browning to visitors, that raised to fever-heat the itching of my palms in his Infant-Samuel-like presence. I have since had reason to think that he would have preferred to be called Billy, and to hunt cats with the other boys in the block: his curls and his poetry were simply another outlet for Mrs. Amyot's irrepressible coquetry.

But if Lancelot was not genuine, his mother's love for him was. It justified everything, the lectures were for the baby, after all. I had not been ten minutes in the room before I was pledged to help Mrs. Amyot carry out her triumphant fraud. If she wanted to lecture on Plato she should—Plato must take his chance like the rest of us! There was no use, of course, in being "discriminating." I preserved sufficient reason to avoid that pitfall, but I suggested "subjects" and made lists of books for her with a fatuity that became more obvious as time attenuated the remembrance of her smile; I even remember thinking that some men might have cut the knot by marrying her, but I handed over Plato as a hostage and escaped by the afternoon train.

The next time I saw her was in New York, when she had become so fashionable that it was a part of the whole duty of woman to be seen at her lectures. The lady who suggested that of course I ought to go and hear Mrs. Amyot, was not very clear about anything except that she was perfectly lovely, and had had a horrid husband, and was doing it to support her boy. The subject of the discourse (I think it was on Ruskin) was clearly of minor importance, not only to my friend, but to the throng of well-dressed and absent-minded ladies who rustled in late, dropped their muffs and pocket-books, and undisguisedly lost themselves in the study of each other's apparel. They received Mrs. Amyot with warmth, but she evidently represented a social obligation like going to church, rather than any more personal interest; in fact, I suspect that every one of the ladies would have remained away, had they been sure that none of the others were coming.

Whether Mrs. Amyot was disheartened by the lack of sympathy between herself and her hearers, or whether the sport of arousing it had become a task, she certainly imparted her platitudes with less convincing warmth than of old. Her voice had the same confidential inflections, but it was like a voice reproduced by a gramophone: the real woman seemed far away. She had grown stouter without losing her dewy freshness, and her smart gown might have been taken to show either the potentialities of a settled income, or a politic concession to the taste of her hearers. As I listened I reproached myself for ever having suspected her of self-deception in saying that she took no pleasure in her work. I was sure now that she did it only for Lancelot, and judging from the size of her audience and the price of the tickets I concluded that Lancelot must be receiving a liberal education.

I was living in New York that winter, and in the rotation of dinners I found myself one evening at Mrs. Amyot's side. The dimple came out at my greeting as punctually as a cuckoo in a Swiss clock, and I detected the same automatic quality in the tone in which she made her usual pretty demand for advice. She was like a musical-box charged with popular airs. They succeeded one another with breathless rapidity, but there was a moment after each when the cylinders scraped and whizzed.

Mrs. Amyot, as I found when I called on her, was living in a sunny flat, with a sitting-room full of flowers and a tea-table that had the air of expecting visitors. She owned that she had been ridiculously successful. It was delightful, of course, on Lancelot's account. Lancelot had been sent to the best school in the country, and if things went well and people didn't tire of his silly mother he was to go to Harvard afterwards. During the next two or three years Mrs. Amyot kept her flat in New York, and radiated art and literature upon the suburbs. I saw her now and then, always stouter, better dressed, more successful and more automatic: she had become a lecturing-machine.

I went abroad for a year or two and when I came back she had disappeared. I asked several people about her, but life had closed over her. She had been last heard of as lecturing, still lecturing, but no one seemed to know when or where.

It was in Boston that I found her at last, forlornly swaying to the oscillations of an overhead strap in a crowded trolley-car. Her face had so changed that I lost myself in a startled reckoning of the time that had elapsed since our parting. She spoke to me shyly, as though aware of my hurried calculation, and conscious that in five years she ought not to have altered so much as to upset my notion of time. Then she seemed to set it down to her dress, for she nervously gathered her cloak over a gown that asked only to be concealed, and shrank into a seat behind the line of prehensile bipeds blocking the aisle of the car.

It was perhaps because she so obviously avoided me that I felt for the first time that I might be of use to her; and when she left the car I made no excuse for following her.

She said nothing of needing advice and did not ask me to walk home with her, concealing, as we talked, her transparent preoccupations under the guise of a sudden interest in all I had been doing since she had last seen me. Of what concerned her, I learned only that Lancelot was well and that for the present she was not lecturing, she was tired and her doctor had ordered her to rest. On the doorstep of a shabby house she paused and held out her hand. She had been so glad to see me and perhaps if I were in Boston again, the tired dimple, as it were, bowed me out and closed the door on the conclusion of the phrase.

Two or three weeks later, at my club in New York, I found a letter from her. In it she owned that she was troubled, that of late she had been unsuccessful, and that, if I chanced to be coming back to Boston, and could spare her a little of that invaluable advice which—A few days later the advice was at her disposal. She told me frankly what had happened. Her public had grown tired of her. She had seen it coming on for some time, and was shrewd enough in detecting the causes. She had more rivals than formerly, younger women, she admitted, with a smile that could still afford to be generous, and then her audiences had grown more critical and consequently more exacting. Lecturing, as she understood it, used to be simple enough. You chose your topic—Raphael, Shakespeare, Gothic Architecture, or some such big familiar "subject"—and read up about it for a week or so at the Athenaeum or the Astor Library, and then told your audience what you had read. Now, it appeared, that simple process was no longer adequate. People had tired of familiar "subjects"; it was the fashion to be interested in things that one hadn't always known about—natural selection, animal magnetism, sociology and comparative folk-lore; while, in literature, the demand had become equally difficult to meet, since Matthew Arnold had introduced the habit of studying the "influence" of one author on another. She had tried lecturing on influences, and had done very well as long as the public was satisfied with the tracing of such obvious influences as that of Turner on Ruskin, of Schiller on Goethe, of Shakespeare on English literature; but such investigations had soon lost all charm for her too-sophisticated audiences, who now demanded either that the influence or the influenced should be quite unknown, or that there should be no perceptible connection between the two. The zest of the performance lay in the measure of ingenuity with which the lecturer established a relation between two people who had probably never heard of each other, much less read each other's works. A pretty Miss Williams with red hair had, for instance, been lecturing with great success on the influence of the Rosicrucians upon the poetry of Keats, while somebody else had given a "course" on the influence of St. Thomas Aquinas upon Professor Huxley.

Mrs. Amyot, warmed by my participation in her distress, went on to say that the growing demand for evolution was what most troubled her. Her grandfather had been a pillar of the Presbyterian ministry, and the idea of her lecturing on Darwin or Herbert Spencer was deeply shocking to her mother and aunts. In one sense the family had staked its literary as well as its spiritual hopes on the literal inspiration of Genesis: what became of "The Fall of Man" in the light of modern exegesis?

The upshot of it was that she had ceased to lecture because she could no longer sell tickets enough to pay for the hire of a lecture-hall; and as for the managers, they wouldn't look at her. She had tried her luck all through the Eastern States and as far south as Washington; but it was of no use, and unless she could get hold of some new subjects, or, better still, of some new audiences, she must simply go out of the business. That would mean the failure of all she had worked for, since Lancelot would have to leave Harvard. She paused, and wept some of the unbecoming tears that spring from real grief. Lancelot, it appeared, was to be a genius. He had passed his opening examinations brilliantly; he had "literary gifts"; he had written beautiful poetry, much of which his mother had copied out, in reverentially slanting characters, in a velvet-bound volume which she drew from a locked drawer.

Lancelot's verse struck me as nothing more alarming than growing-pains; but it was not to learn this that she had summoned me. What she wanted was to be assured that he was worth working for, an assurance which I managed to convey by the simple stratagem of remarking that the poems reminded me of Swinburne, and so they did, as well as of Browning, Tennyson, Rossetti, and all the other poets who supply young authors with original inspirations.

This point being established, it remained to be decided by what means his mother was, in the French phrase, to pay herself the luxury of a poet. It was clear that this indulgence could be bought only with counterfeit coin, and that the one way of helping Mrs. Amyot was to become a party to the circulation of such currency. My fetish of intellectual integrity went down like a ninepin before the appeal of a woman no longer young and distinctly foolish, but full of those dear contradictions and irrelevancies that will always make flesh and blood prevail against a syllogism. When I took leave of Mrs. Amyot I had promised her a dozen letters to Western universities and had half pledged myself to sketch out a lecture on the reconciliation of science and religion.

In the West she achieved a success which for a year or more embittered my perusal of the morning papers. The fascination that lures the murderer back to the scene of his crime drew my eye to every paragraph celebrating Mrs. Amyot's last brilliant lecture on the influence of something upon somebody; and her own letters, she overwhelmed me with them, spared me no detail of the entertainment given in her honor by the Palimpsest Club of Omaha or of her reception at the University of Leadville. The college professors were especially kind: she assured me that she had never before met with such discriminating sympathy. I winced at the adjective, which cast a sudden light on the vast machinery of fraud that I had set in motion. All over my native land, men of hitherto unblemished integrity were conniving with me in urging their friends to go and hear Mrs. Amyot lecture on the reconciliation of science and religion! My only hope was that, somewhere among the number of my accomplices, Mrs. Amyot might find one who would marry her in the defense of his convictions.

None, apparently, resorted to such heroic measures; for about two years later I was startled by the announcement that Mrs. Amyot was lecturing in Trenton, New Jersey, on modern theosophy in the light of the Vedas. The following week she was at Newark, discussing Schopenhauer in the light of recent psychology. The week after that I was on the deck of an ocean steamer, reconsidering my share in Mrs. Amyot's triumphs with the impartiality with which one views an episode that is being left behind at the rate of twenty knots an hour. After all, I had been helping a mother to educate her son.

The next ten years of my life were spent in Europe, and when I came home the recollection of Mrs. Amyot had become as inoffensive as one of those pathetic ghosts who are said to strive in vain to make themselves visible to the living. I did not even notice the fact that I no longer heard her spoken of; she had dropped like a dead leaf from the bough of memory.

A year or two after my return I was condemned to one of the worst punishments a worker can undergo, an enforced holiday. The doctors who pronounced the inhuman sentence decreed that it should be worked out in the South, and for a whole winter I carried my cough, my thermometer and my idleness from one fashionable orange-grove to another. In the vast and melancholy sea of my disoccupation I clutched like a drowning man at any human driftwood within reach. I took a critical and depreciatory interest in the coughs, the thermometers and the idleness of my fellow-sufferers; but to the healthy, the occupied, the transient I clung with undiscriminating enthusiasm.

In no other way can I explain, as I look back on it, the importance I attached to the leisurely confidences of a new arrival with a brown beard who, tilted back at my side on a hotel veranda hung with roses, imparted to me one afternoon the simple annals of his past. There was nothing in the tale to kindle the most inflammable imagination, and though the man had a pleasant frank face and a voice differing agreeably from the shrill inflections of our fellow-lodgers, it is probable that under different conditions his discursive history of successful business ventures in a Western city would have affected me somewhat in the manner of a lullaby.

Even at the tune I was not sure I liked his agreeable voice: it had a self-importance out of keeping with the humdrum nature of his story, as though a breeze engaged in shaking out a table-cloth should have fancied itself inflating a banner. But this criticism may have been a mere mark of my own fastidiousness, for the man seemed a simple fellow, satisfied with his middling fortunes, and already (he was not much past thirty) deep-sunk in conjugal content.

He had just started on an anecdote connected with the cutting of his eldest boy's teeth, when a lady I knew, returning from her late drive, paused before us for a moment in the twilight, with the smile which is the feminine equivalent of beads to savages.

"Won't you take a ticket?" she said sweetly.

Of course I would take a ticket, but for what? I ventured to inquire.

"Oh, that's so good of you, for the lecture this evening. You needn't go, you know; we're none of us going; most of us have been through it already at Aiken and at Saint Augustine and at Palm Beach. I've given away my tickets to some new people who've just come from the North, and some of us are going to send our maids, just to fill up the room."

"And may I ask to whom you are going to pay this delicate attention?"

"Oh, I thought you knew, to poor Mrs. Amyot. She's been lecturing all over the South this winter; she's simply haunted me ever since I left New York, and we had six weeks of her at Bar Harbor last summer! One has to take tickets, you know, because she's a widow and does it for her son, to pay for his education. She's so plucky and nice about it, and talks about him in such a touching unaffected way, that everybody is sorry for her, and we all simply ruin ourselves in tickets. I do hope that boy's nearly educated!"

"Mrs. Amyot? Mrs. Amyot?" I repeated. "Is she still educating her son?"

"Oh, do you know about her? Has she been at it long? There's some comfort in that, for I suppose when the boy's provided for the poor thing will be able to take a rest, and give us one!"

She laughed and held out her hand.

"Here's your ticket. Did you say tickets—two? Oh, thanks. Of course you needn't go."

"But I mean to go. Mrs. Amyot is an old friend of mine."

"Do you really? That's awfully good of you. Perhaps I'll go too if I can persuade Charlie and the others to come. And I wonder"—in a well-directed aside—"if your friend—?"

I telegraphed her under cover of the dusk that my friend was of too recent standing to be drawn into her charitable toils, and she masked her mistake under a rattle of friendly adjurations not to be late, and to be sure to keep a seat for her, as she had quite made up her mind to go even if Charlie and the others wouldn't.

The flutter of her skirts subsided in the distance, and my neighbor, who had half turned away to light a cigar, made no effort to reopen the conversation. At length, fearing he might have overheard the allusion to himself, I ventured to ask if he were going to the lecture that evening.

"Much obliged—I have a ticket," he said abruptly.

This struck me as in such bad taste that I made no answer; and it was he who spoke next.

"Did I understand you to say that you were an old friend of Mrs. Amyot's?"

"I think I may claim to be, if it is the same Mrs. Amyot I had the pleasure of knowing many years ago. My Mrs. Amyot used to lecture too—"

"To pay for her son's education?"

"I believe so."

"Well—see you later."

He got up and walked into the house.

In the hotel drawing-room that evening there was but a meagre sprinkling of guests, among whom I saw my brown-bearded friend sitting alone on a sofa, with his head against the wall. It could not have been curiosity to see Mrs. Amyot that had impelled him to attend the performance, for it would have been impossible for him, without changing his place, to command the improvised platform at the end of the room. When I looked at him he seemed lost in contemplation of the chandelier.

The lady from whom I had bought my tickets fluttered in late, unattended by Charlie and the others, and assuring me that she would scream if we had the lecture on Ibsen—she had heard it three times already that winter. A glance at the programme reassured her: it informed us (in the lecturer's own slanting hand) that Mrs. Amyot was to lecture on the Cosmogony.

After a long pause, during which the small audience coughed and moved its chairs and showed signs of regretting that it had come, the door opened, and Mrs. Amyot stepped upon the platform. Ah, poor lady!

Someone said "Hush!", the coughing and chair-shifting subsided, and she began.

It was like looking at one's self early in the morning in a cracked mirror. I had no idea I had grown so old. As for Lancelot, he must have a beard. A beard? The word struck me, and without knowing why I glanced across the room at my bearded friend on the sofa. Oddly enough he was looking at me, with a half-defiant, half-sullen expression; and as our glances crossed, and his fell, the conviction came to me that he was Lancelot.

I don't remember a word of the lecture; and yet there were enough of them to have filled a good-sized dictionary. The stream of Mrs. Amyot's eloquence had become a flood: one had the despairing sense that she had sprung a leak, and that until the plumber came there was nothing to be done about it.

The plumber came at length, in the shape of a clock striking ten; my companion, with a sigh of relief, drifted away in search of Charlie and the others; the audience scattered with the precipitation of people who had discharged a duty; and, without surprise, I found the brown-bearded stranger at my elbow.

We stood alone in the bare-floored room, under the flaring chandelier.

"I think you told me this afternoon that you were an old friend of Mrs. Amyot's?" he began awkwardly.

I assented.

"Will you come in and see her?"

"Now? I shall be very glad to, if—"

"She's ready; she's expecting you," he interposed.

He offered no further explanation, and I followed him in silence. He led me down the long corridor, and pushed open the door of a sitting-room.

"Mother," he said, closing the door after we had entered, "here's the gentleman who says he used to know you."

Mrs. Amyot, who sat in an easy-chair stirring a cup of bouillon, looked up with a start. She had evidently not seen me in the audience, and her son's description had failed to convey my identity. I saw a frightened look in her eyes; then, like a frost flower on a window-pane, the dimple expanded on her wrinkled cheek, and she held out her hand.

"I'm so glad," she said, "so glad!"

She turned to her son, who stood watching us. "You must have told Lancelot all about me, you've known me so long!"

"I haven't had time to talk to your son, since I knew he was your son," I explained.

Her brow cleared. "Then you haven't had time to say anything very dreadful?" she said with a laugh.

"It is he who has been saying dreadful things," I returned, trying to fall in with her tone.

I saw my mistake. "What things?" she faltered.

"Making me feel how old I am by telling me about his children."

"My grandchildren!" she exclaimed with a blush.

"Well, if you choose to put it so."

She laughed again, vaguely, and was silent. I hesitated a moment and then put out my hand.

"I see you are tired. I shouldn't have ventured to come in at this hour if your son—"

The son stepped between us. "Yes, I asked him to come," he said to his mother, in his clear self-assertive voice. "I haven't told him anything yet; but you've got to—now. That's what I brought him for."

His mother straightened herself, but I saw her eye waver.

"Lancelot—" she began.

"Mr. Amyot," I said, turning to the young man, "if your mother will let me come back to-morrow, I shall be very glad—"

He struck his hand hard against the table on which he was leaning.

"No, sir! It won't take long, but it's got to be said now."

He moved nearer to his mother, and I saw his lip twitch under his beard. After all, he was younger and less sure of himself than I had fancied.

"See here, mother," he went on, "there's something here that's got to be cleared up, and as you say this gentleman is an old friend of yours it had better be cleared up in his presence. Maybe he can help explain it—and if he can't, it's got to be explained to him."

Mrs. Amyot's lips moved, but she made no sound. She glanced at me helplessly and sat down. My early inclination to thrash Lancelot was beginning to reassert itself. I took up my hat and moved toward the door.

"Mrs. Amyot is under no obligation to explain anything whatever to me," I said curtly.

"Well! She's under an obligation to me, then, to explain something in your presence." He turned to her again. "Do you know what the people in this hotel are saying? Do you know what he thinks, what they all think? That you're doing this lecturing to support me, to pay for my education! They say you go round telling them so. That's what they buy the tickets for—they do it out of charity. Ask him if it isn't what they say—ask him if they weren't joking about it on the piazza before dinner. The others think I'm a little boy, but he's known you for years, and he must have known how old I was. He must have known it wasn't to pay for my education!"

He stood before her with his hands clenched, the veins beating in his temples. She had grown very pale, and her cheeks looked hollow. When she spoke her voice had an odd click in it.

"If, if these ladies and gentlemen have been coming to my lectures out of charity, I see nothing to be ashamed of in that—" she faltered.

"If they've been coming out of charity to me," he retorted, "don't you see you've been making me a party to a fraud? Isn't there any shame in that?" His forehead reddened. "Mother! Can't you see the shame of letting people think I was a deadbeat, who sponged on you for my keep? Let alone making us both the laughing-stock of every place you go to!"

"I never did that, Lancelot!"

"Did what?"

"Made you a laughing-stock—"

He stepped close to her and caught her wrist.

"Will you look me in the face and swear you never told people you were doing this lecturing business to support me?"

There was a long silence. He dropped her wrist and she lifted a limp handkerchief to her frightened eyes. "I did do it, to support you, to educate you"—she sobbed.

"We're not talking about what you did when I was a boy. Everybody who knows me knows I've been a grateful son. Have I ever taken a penny from you since I left college ten years ago?"

"I never said you had! How can you accuse your mother of such wickedness, Lancelot?"

"Have you never told anybody in this hotel, or anywhere else in the last ten years, that you were lecturing to support me? Answer me that!"

"How can you," she wept, "before a stranger?"

"Haven't you said such things about me to strangers?" he retorted.

"Lancelot!"

"Well, answer me, then. Say you haven't, mother!" His voice broke unexpectedly and he took her hand with a gentler touch. "I'll believe anything you tell me," he said almost humbly.

She mistook his tone and raised her head with a rash clutch at dignity.

"I think you'd better ask this gentleman to excuse you first."

"No, by God, I won't!" he cried. "This gentleman says he knows all about you and I mean him to know all about me too. I don't mean that he or anybody else under this roof shall go on thinking for another twenty-four hours that a cent of their money has ever gone into my pockets since I was old enough to shift for myself. And he sha'n't leave this room till you've made that clear to him."

He stepped back as he spoke and put his shoulders against the door.

"My dear young gentleman," I said politely, "I shall leave this room exactly when I see fit to do so, and that is now. I have already told you that Mrs. Amyot owes me no explanation of her conduct."

"But I owe you an explanation of mine, you and everyone who has bought a single one of her lecture tickets. Do you suppose a man who's been through what I went through while that woman was talking to you in the porch before dinner is going to hold his tongue, and not attempt to justify himself? No decent man is going to sit down under that sort of thing. It's enough to ruin his character. If you're my mother's friend, you owe it to me to hear what I've got to say."

He pulled out his handkerchief and wiped his forehead.

"Good God, mother!" he burst out suddenly, "what did you do it for? Haven't you had everything you wanted ever since I was able to pay for it? Haven't I paid you back every cent you spent on me when I was in college? Have I ever gone back on you since I was big enough to work?" He turned to me with a laugh. "I thought she did it to amuse herself, and because there was such a demand for her lectures. Such a demand! That's what she always told me. When we asked her to come out and spend this winter with us in Minneapolis, she wrote back that she couldn't because she had engagements all through the south, and her manager wouldn't let her off. That's the reason why I came all the way on here to see her. We thought she was the most popular lecturer in the United States, my wife and I did! We were awfully proud of it too, I can tell you." He dropped into a chair, still laughing.

"How can you, Lancelot, how can you!" His mother, forgetful of my presence, was clinging to him with tentative caresses. "When you didn't need the money any longer I spent it all on the children, you know I did."

"Yes, on lace christening dresses and life-size rocking-horses with real manes! The kind of thing children can't do without."

"Oh, Lancelot, Lancelot, I loved them so! How can you believe such falsehoods about me?"

"What falsehoods about you?"

"That I ever told anybody such dreadful things?"

He put her back gently, keeping his eyes on hers. "Did you never tell anybody in this house that you were lecturing to support your son?"

Her hands dropped from his shoulders and she flashed round on me in sudden anger.

"I know what I think of people who call themselves friends and who come between a mother and her son!"

"Oh, mother, mother!" he groaned.

I went up to him and laid my hand on his shoulder.

"My dear man," I said, "don't you see the uselessness of prolonging this?"

"Yes, I do," he answered abruptly; and before I could forestall his movement he rose and walked out of the room.

There was a long silence, measured by the lessening reverberations of his footsteps down the wooden floor of the corridor.

When they ceased I approached Mrs. Amyot, who had sunk into her chair. I held out my hand and she took it without a trace of resentment on her ravaged face.

"I sent his wife a seal-skin jacket at Christmas!" she said, with the tears running down her cheeks.

SOULS BELATED

I

Their railway-carriage had been full when the train left Bologna; but at the first station beyond Milan their only remaining companion, a courtly person who ate garlic out of a carpet-bag, had left his crumb-strewn seat with a bow.

Lydia's eye regretfully followed the shiny broadcloth of his retreating back till it lost itself in the cloud of touts and cab-drivers hanging about the station; then she glanced across at Gannett and caught the same regret in his look. They were both sorry to be alone.

"Par-ten-za!" shouted the guard. The train vibrated to a sudden slamming of doors; a waiter ran along the platform with a tray of fossilized sandwiches; a belated porter flung a bundle of shawls and band-boxes into a third-class carriage; the guard snapped out a brief Partensa! which indicated the purely ornamental nature of his first shout; and the train swung out of the station.

The direction of the road had changed, and a shaft of sunlight struck across the dusty red velvet seats into Lydia's corner. Gannett did not notice it. He had returned to his Revue de Paris, and she had to rise and lower the shade of the farther window. Against the vast horizon of their leisure such incidents stood out sharply.

Having lowered the shade, Lydia sat down, leaving the length of the carriage between herself and Gannett. At length he missed her and looked up.

"I moved out of the sun," she hastily explained.

He looked at her curiously: the sun was beating on her through the shade.

"Very well," he said pleasantly; adding, "You don't mind?" as he drew a cigarette-case from his pocket.

It was a refreshing touch, relieving the tension of her spirit with the suggestion that, after all, if he could smoke—! The relief was only momentary. Her experience of smokers was limited (her husband had disapproved of the use of tobacco) but she knew from hearsay that men sometimes smoked to get away from things; that a cigar might be the masculine equivalent of darkened windows and a headache. Gannett, after a puff or two, returned to his review.

It was just as she had foreseen; he feared to speak as much as she did. It was one of the misfortunes of their situation that they were never busy enough to necessitate, or even to justify, the postponement of unpleasant discussions. If they avoided a question it was obviously, unconcealably because the question was disagreeable. They had unlimited leisure and an accumulation of mental energy to devote to any subject that presented itself; new topics were in fact at a premium. Lydia sometimes had premonitions of a famine-stricken period when there would be nothing left to talk about, and she had already caught herself doling out piecemeal what, in the first prodigality of their confidences, she would have flung to him in a breath. Their silence therefore might simply mean that they had nothing to say; but it was another disadvantage of their position that it allowed infinite opportunity for the classification of minute differences. Lydia had learned to distinguish between real and factitious silences; and under Gannett's she now detected a hum of speech to which her own thoughts made breathless answer.

How could it be otherwise, with that thing between them? She glanced up at the rack overhead. The thing was there, in her dressing-bag, symbolically suspended over her head and his. He was thinking of it now, just as she was; they had been thinking of it in unison ever since they had entered the train. While the carriage had held other travellers they had screened her from his thoughts; but now that he and she were alone she knew exactly what was passing through his mind; she could almost hear him asking himself what he should say to her....

The thing had come that morning, brought up to her in an innocent-looking envelope with the rest of their letters, as they were leaving the hotel at Bologna. As she tore it open, she and Gannett were laughing over some ineptitude of the local guide-book, they had been driven, of late, to make the most of such incidental humors of travel. Even when she had unfolded the document she took it for some unimportant business paper sent abroad for her signature, and her eye travelled inattentively over the curly Whereases of the preamble until a word arrested her:—Divorce. There it stood, an impassable barrier, between her husband's name and hers.

She had been prepared for it, of course, as healthy people are said to be prepared for death, in the sense of knowing it must come without in the least expecting that it will. She had known from the first that Tillotson meant to divorce her, but what did it matter? Nothing mattered, in those first days of supreme deliverance, but the fact that she was free; and not so much (she had begun to be aware) that freedom had released her from Tillotson as that it had given her to Gannett. This discovery had not been agreeable to her self-esteem. She had preferred to think that Tillotson had himself embodied all her reasons for leaving him; and those he represented had seemed cogent enough to stand in no need of reinforcement. Yet she had not left him till she met Gannett. It was her love for Gannett that had made life with Tillotson so poor and incomplete a business. If she had never, from the first, regarded her marriage as a full cancelling of her claims upon life, she had at least, for a number of years, accepted it as a provisional compensation, she had made it "do." Existence in the commodious Tillotson mansion in Fifth Avenue, with Mrs. Tillotson senior commanding the approaches from the second-story front windows—had been reduced to a series of purely automatic acts. The moral atmosphere of the Tillotson interior was as carefully screened and curtained as the house itself: Mrs. Tillotson senior dreaded ideas as much as a draught in her back. Prudent people liked an even temperature; and to do anything unexpected was as foolish as going out in the rain. One of the chief advantages of being rich was that one need not be exposed to unforeseen contingencies: by the use of ordinary firmness and common sense one could make sure of doing exactly the same thing every day at the same hour. These doctrines, reverentially imbibed with his mother's milk, Tillotson (a model son who had never given his parents an hour's anxiety) complacently expounded to his wife, testifying to his sense of their importance by the regularity with which he wore goloshes on damp days, his punctuality at meals, and his elaborate precautions against burglars and contagious diseases. Lydia, coming from a smaller town, and entering New York life through the portals of the Tillotson mansion, had mechanically accepted this point of view as inseparable from having a front pew in church and a parterre box at the opera. All the people who came to the house revolved in the same small circle of prejudices. It was the kind of society in which, after dinner, the ladies compared the exorbitant charges of their children's teachers, and agreed that, even with the new duties on French clothes, it was cheaper in the end to get everything from Worth; while the husbands, over their cigars, lamented municipal corruption, and decided that the men to start a reform were those who had no private interests at stake.

To Lydia this view of life had become a matter of course, just as lumbering about in her mother-in-law's landau had come to seem the only possible means of locomotion, and listening every Sunday to a fashionable Presbyterian divine the inevitable atonement for having thought oneself bored on the other six days of the week. Before she met Gannett her life had seemed merely dull: his coming made it appear like one of those dismal Cruikshank prints in which the people are all ugly and all engaged in occupations that are either vulgar or stupid.

It was natural that Tillotson should be the chief sufferer from this readjustment of focus. Gannett's nearness had made her husband ridiculous, and a part of the ridicule had been reflected on herself. Her tolerance laid her open to a suspicion of obtuseness from which she must, at all costs, clear herself in Gannett's eyes.

She did not understand this until afterwards. At the time she fancied that she had merely reached the limits of endurance. In so large a charter of liberties as the mere act of leaving Tillotson seemed to confer, the small question of divorce or no divorce did not count. It was when she saw that she had left her husband only to be with Gannett that she perceived the significance of anything affecting their relations. Her husband, in casting her off, had virtually flung her at Gannett: it was thus that the world viewed it. The measure of alacrity with which Gannett would receive her would be the subject of curious speculation over afternoon-tea tables and in club corners. She knew what would be said—she had heard it so often of others! The recollection bathed her in misery. The men would probably back Gannett to "do the decent thing"; but the ladies' eye-brows would emphasize the worthlessness of such enforced fidelity; and after all, they would be right. She had put herself in a position where Gannett "owed" her something; where, as a gentleman, he was bound to "stand the damage." The idea of accepting such compensation had never crossed her mind; the so-called rehabilitation of such a marriage had always seemed to her the only real disgrace. What she dreaded was the necessity of having to explain herself; of having to combat his arguments; of calculating, in spite of herself, the exact measure of insistence with which he pressed them. She knew not whether she most shrank from his insisting too much or too little. In such a case the nicest sense of proportion might be at fault; and how easy to fall into the error of taking her resistance for a test of his sincerity! Whichever way she turned, an ironical implication confronted her: she had the exasperated sense of having walked into the trap of some stupid practical joke.

Beneath all these preoccupations lurked the dread of what he was thinking. Sooner or later, of course, he would have to speak; but that, in the meantime, he should think, even for a moment, that there was any use in speaking, seemed to her simply unendurable. Her sensitiveness on this point was aggravated by another fear, as yet barely on the level of consciousness; the fear of unwillingly involving Gannett in the trammels of her dependence. To look upon him as the instrument of her liberation; to resist in herself the least tendency to a wifely taking possession of his future; had seemed to Lydia the one way of maintaining the dignity of their relation. Her view had not changed, but she was aware of a growing inability to keep her thoughts fixed on the essential point—the point of parting with Gannett. It was easy to face as long as she kept it sufficiently far off: but what was this act of mental postponement but a gradual encroachment on his future? What was needful was the courage to recognize the moment when, by some word or look, their voluntary fellowship should be transformed into a bondage the more wearing that it was based on none of those common obligations which make the most imperfect marriage in some sort a centre of gravity.

When the porter, at the next station, threw the door open, Lydia drew back, making way for the hoped-for intruder; but none came, and the train took up its leisurely progress through the spring wheat-fields and budding copses. She now began to hope that Gannett would speak before the next station. She watched him furtively, half-disposed to return to the seat opposite his, but there was an artificiality about his absorption that restrained her. She had never before seen him read with so conspicuous an air of warding off interruption. What could he be thinking of? Why should he be afraid to speak? Or was it her answer that he dreaded?

The train paused for the passing of an express, and he put down his book and leaned out of the window. Presently he turned to her with a smile. "There's a jolly old villa out here," he said.

His easy tone relieved her, and she smiled back at him as she crossed over to his corner.

Beyond the embankment, through the opening in a mossy wall, she caught sight of the villa, with its broken balustrades, its stagnant fountains, and the stone satyr closing the perspective of a dusky grass-walk.

"How should you like to live there?" he asked as the train moved on.

"There?"

"In some such place, I mean. One might do worse, don't you think so? There must be at least two centuries of solitude under those yew-trees. Shouldn't you like it?"

"I—I don't know," she faltered. She knew now that he meant to speak.

He lit another cigarette. "We shall have to live somewhere, you know," he said as he bent above the match.

Lydia tried to speak carelessly. "Je n'en vois pas la necessite! Why not live everywhere, as we have been doing?"

"But we can't travel forever, can we?"

"Oh, forever's a long word," she objected, picking up the review he had thrown aside.

"For the rest of our lives then," he said, moving nearer.

She made a slight gesture which caused his hand to slip from hers.

"Why should we make plans? I thought you agreed with me that it's pleasanter to drift."

He looked at her hesitatingly. "It's been pleasant, certainly; but I suppose I shall have to get at my work again some day. You know I haven't written a line since—all this time," he hastily emended.

She flamed with sympathy and self-reproach. "Oh, if you mean that, if you want to write, of course we must settle down. How stupid of me not to have thought of it sooner! Where shall we go? Where do you think you could work best? We oughtn't to lose any more time."

He hesitated again. "I had thought of a villa in these parts. It's quiet; we shouldn't be bothered. Should you like it?"

"Of course I should like it." She paused and looked away. "But I thought—I remember your telling me once that your best work had been done in a crowd—in big cities. Why should you shut yourself up in a desert?"

Gannett, for a moment, made no reply. At length he said, avoiding her eye as carefully as she avoided his: "It might be different now; I can't tell, of course, till I try. A writer ought not to be dependent on his milieu; it's a mistake to humor oneself in that way; and I thought that just at first you might prefer to be—"

She faced him. "To be what?"

"Well—quiet. I mean—"

"What do you mean by 'at first'?" she interrupted.

He paused again. "I mean after we are married."

She thrust up her chin and turned toward the window. "Thank you!" she tossed back at him.

"Lydia!" he exclaimed blankly; and she felt in every fibre of her averted person that he had made the inconceivable, the unpardonable mistake of anticipating her acquiescence.

The train rattled on and he groped for a third cigarette. Lydia remained silent.

"I haven't offended you?" he ventured at length, in the tone of a man who feels his way.

She shook her head with a sigh. "I thought you understood," she moaned. Their eyes met and she moved back to his side.

"Do you want to know how not to offend me? By taking it for granted, once for all, that you've said your say on this odious question and that I've said mine, and that we stand just where we did this morning before that—that hateful paper came to spoil everything between us!"

"To spoil everything between us? What on earth do you mean? Aren't you glad to be free?"

"I was free before."

"Not to marry me," he suggested.

"But I don't want to marry you!" she cried.

She saw that he turned pale. "I'm obtuse, I suppose," he said slowly. "I confess I don't see what you're driving at. Are you tired of the whole business? Or was I simply a—an excuse for getting away? Perhaps you didn't care to travel alone? Was that it? And now you want to chuck me?" His voice had grown harsh. "You owe me a straight answer, you know; don't be tender-hearted!"

Her eyes swam as she leaned to him. "Don't you see it's because I care—because I care so much? Oh, Ralph! Can't you see how it would humiliate me? Try to feel it as a woman would! Don't you see the misery of being made your wife in this way? If I'd known you as a girl, that would have been a real marriage! But now, this vulgar fraud upon society, and upon a society we despised and laughed at, this sneaking back into a position that we've voluntarily forfeited: don't you see what a cheap compromise it is? We neither of us believe in the abstract 'sacredness' of marriage; we both know that no ceremony is needed to consecrate our love for each other; what object can we have in marrying, except the secret fear of each that the other may escape, or the secret longing to work our way back gradually, oh, very gradually, into the esteem of the people whose conventional morality we have always ridiculed and hated? And the very fact that, after a decent interval, these same people would come and dine with us, the women who talk about the indissolubility of marriage, and who would let me die in a gutter to-day because I am 'leading a life of sin'—doesn't that disgust you more than their turning their backs on us now? I can stand being cut by them, but I couldn't stand their coming to call and asking what I meant to do about visiting that unfortunate Mrs. So-and-so!"

She paused, and Gannett maintained a perplexed silence.

"You judge things too theoretically," he said at length, slowly. "Life is made up of compromises."

"The life we ran away from—yes! If we had been willing to accept them"—she flushed—"we might have gone on meeting each other at Mrs. Tillotson's dinners."

He smiled slightly. "I didn't know that we ran away to found a new system of ethics. I supposed it was because we loved each other."

"Life is complex, of course; isn't it the very recognition of that fact that separates us from the people who see it tout d'une pièce? If they are right—if marriage is sacred in itself and the individual must always be sacrificed to the family—then there can be no real marriage between us, since our—our being together is a protest against the sacrifice of the individual to the family." She interrupted herself with a laugh. "You'll say now that I'm giving you a lecture on sociology! Of course one acts as one can, as one must, perhaps—pulled by all sorts of invisible threads; but at least one needn't pretend, for social advantages, to subscribe to a creed that ignores the complexity of human motives—that classifies people by arbitrary signs, and puts it in everybody's reach to be on Mrs. Tillotson's visiting-list. It may be necessary that the world should be ruled by conventions, but if we believed in them, why did we break through them? And if we don't believe in them, is it honest to take advantage of the protection they afford?"

Gannett hesitated. "One may believe in them or not; but as long as they do rule the world it is only by taking advantage of their protection that one can find a modus vivendi."

"Do outlaws need a modus vivendi?"

He looked at her hopelessly. Nothing is more perplexing to man than the mental process of a woman who reasons her emotions.

She thought she had scored a point and followed it up passionately. "You do understand, don't you? You see how the very thought of the thing humiliates me! We are together to-day because we choose to be, don't let us look any farther than that!" She caught his hands. "Promise me you'll never speak of it again; promise me you'll never think of it even," she implored, with a tearful prodigality of italics.

Through what followed, his protests, his arguments, his final unconvinced submission to her wishes, she had a sense of his but half-discerning all that, for her, had made the moment so tumultuous. They had reached that memorable point in every heart-history when, for the first time, the man seems obtuse and the woman irrational. It was the abundance of his intentions that consoled her, on reflection, for what they lacked in quality. After all, it would have been worse, incalculably worse, to have detected any over-readiness to understand her.

II

When the train at night-fall brought them to their journey's end at the edge of one of the lakes, Lydia was glad that they were not, as usual, to pass from one solitude to another. Their wanderings during the year had indeed been like the flight of outlaws: through Sicily, Dalmatia, Transylvania and Southern Italy they had persisted in their tacit avoidance of their kind. Isolation, at first, had deepened the flavor of their happiness, as night intensifies the scent of certain flowers; but in the new phase on which they were entering, Lydia's chief wish was that they should be less abnormally exposed to the action of each other's thoughts.

She shrank, nevertheless, as the brightly-looming bulk of the fashionable Anglo-American hotel on the water's brink began to radiate toward their advancing boat its vivid suggestion of social order, visitors' lists, Church services, and the bland inquisition of the table-d'hote. The mere fact that in a moment or two she must take her place on the hotel register as Mrs. Gannett seemed to weaken the springs of her resistance.

They had meant to stay for a night only, on their way to a lofty village among the glaciers of Monte Rosa; but after the first plunge into publicity, when they entered the dining-room, Lydia felt the relief of being lost in a crowd, of ceasing for a moment to be the centre of Gannett's scrutiny; and in his face she caught the reflection of her feeling. After dinner, when she went upstairs, he strolled into the smoking-room, and an hour or two later, sitting in the darkness of her window, she heard his voice below and saw him walking up and down the terrace with a companion cigar at his side. When he came up he told her he had been talking to the hotel chaplain, a very good sort of fellow.

"Queer little microcosms, these hotels! Most of these people live here all summer and then migrate to Italy or the Riviera. The English are the only people who can lead that kind of life with dignity, those soft-voiced old ladies in Shetland shawls somehow carry the British Empire under their caps. Civis Romanus sum. It's a curious study, there might be some good things to work up here."

He stood before her with the vivid preoccupied stare of the novelist on the trail of a "subject." With a relief that was half painful she noticed that, for the first time since they had been together, he was hardly aware of her presence. "Do you think you could write here?"

"Here? I don't know." His stare dropped. "After being out of things so long one's first impressions are bound to be tremendously vivid, you know. I see a dozen threads already that one might follow—"

He broke off with a touch of embarrassment.

"Then follow them. We'll stay," she said with sudden decision.

"Stay here?" He glanced at her in surprise, and then, walking to the window, looked out upon the dusky slumber of the garden.

"Why not?" she said at length, in a tone of veiled irritation.

"The place is full of old cats in caps who gossip with the chaplain. Shall you like—I mean, it would be different if—"

She flamed up.

"Do you suppose I care? It's none of their business."

"Of course not; but you won't get them to think so."

"They may think what they please."

He looked at her doubtfully.

"It's for you to decide."

"We'll stay," she repeated.

Gannett, before they met, had made himself known as a successful writer of short stories and of a novel which had achieved the distinction of being widely discussed. The reviewers called him "promising," and Lydia now accused herself of having too long interfered with the fulfilment of his promise. There was a special irony in the fact, since his passionate assurances that only the stimulus of her companionship could bring out his latent faculty had almost given the dignity of a "vocation" to her course: there had been moments when she had felt unable to assume, before posterity, the responsibility of thwarting his career. And, after all, he had not written a line since they had been together: his first desire to write had come from renewed contact with the world! Was it all a mistake then? Must the most intelligent choice work more disastrously than the blundering combinations of chance? Or was there a still more humiliating answer to her perplexities? His sudden impulse of activity so exactly coincided with her own wish to withdraw, for a time, from the range of his observation, that she wondered if he too were not seeking sanctuary from intolerable problems.

"You must begin to-morrow!" she cried, hiding a tremor under the laugh with which she added, "I wonder if there's any ink in the inkstand?"

Whatever else they had at the Hotel Bellosguardo, they had, as Miss Pinsent said, "a certain tone." It was to Lady Susan Condit that they owed this inestimable benefit; an advantage ranking in Miss Pinsent's opinion above even the lawn tennis courts and the resident chaplain. It was the fact of Lady Susan's annual visit that made the hotel what it was. Miss Pinsent was certainly the last to underrate such a privilege:—"It's so important, my dear, forming as we do a little family, that there should be someone to give the tone; and no one could do it better than Lady Susan—an earl's daughter and a person of such determination. Dear Mrs. Ainger now, who really ought, you know, when Lady Susan's away, absolutely refuses to assert herself." Miss Pinsent sniffed derisively. "A bishop's niece!—my dear, I saw her once actually give in to some South Americans, and before us all. She gave up her seat at table to oblige them, such a lack of dignity! Lady Susan spoke to her very plainly about it afterwards."

Miss Pinsent glanced across the lake and adjusted her auburn front.

"But of course I don't deny that the stand Lady Susan takes is not always easy to live up to, for the rest of us, I mean. Monsieur Grossart, our good proprietor, finds it trying at times, I know, he has said as much, privately, to Mrs. Ainger and me. After all, the poor man is not to blame for wanting to fill his hotel, is he? And Lady Susan is so difficult, so very difficult, about new people. One might almost say that she disapproves of them beforehand, on principle. And yet she's had warnings, she very nearly made a dreadful mistake once with the Duchess of Levens, who dyed her hair and—well, swore and smoked. One would have thought that might have been a lesson to Lady Susan." Miss Pinsent resumed her knitting with a sigh. "There are exceptions, of course. She took at once to you and Mr. Gannett—it was quite remarkable, really. Oh, I don't mean that either, of course not! It was perfectly natural, we all thought you so charming and interesting from the first day, we knew at once that Mr. Gannett was intellectual, by the magazines you took in; but you know what I mean. Lady Susan is so very—well, I won't say prejudiced, as Mrs. Ainger does—but so prepared not to like new people, that her taking to you in that way was a surprise to us all, I confess."

Miss Pinsent sent a significant glance down the long laurustinus alley from the other end of which two people, a lady and gentleman, were strolling toward them through the smiling neglect of the garden.

"In this case, of course, it's very different; that I'm willing to admit. Their looks are against them; but, as Mrs. Ainger says, one can't exactly tell them so."

"She's very handsome," Lydia ventured, with her eyes on the lady, who showed, under the dome of a vivid sunshade, the hour-glass figure and superlative coloring of a Christmas chromo.

"That's the worst of it. She's too handsome."

"Well, after all, she can't help that."

"Other people manage to," said Miss Pinsent skeptically.

"But isn't it rather unfair of Lady Susan, considering that nothing is known about them?"

"But, my dear, that's the very thing that's against them. It's infinitely worse than any actual knowledge."

Lydia mentally agreed that, in the case of Mrs. Linton, it possibly might be.

"I wonder why they came here?" she mused.

"That's against them too. It's always a bad sign when loud people come to a quiet place. And they've brought van-loads of boxes, her maid told Mrs. Ainger's that they meant to stop indefinitely."

"And Lady Susan actually turned her back on her in the salon?"

"My dear, she said it was for our sakes: that makes it so unanswerable! But poor Grossart is in a way! The Lintons have taken his most expensive suite, you know, the yellow damask drawing-room above the portico, and they have champagne with every meal!"

They were silent as Mr. and Mrs. Linton sauntered by; the lady with tempestuous brows and challenging chin; the gentleman, a blond stripling, trailing after her, head downward, like a reluctant child dragged by his nurse.

"What does your husband think of them, my dear?" Miss Pinsent whispered as they passed out of earshot.

Lydia stooped to pick a violet in the border.

"He hasn't told me."

"Of your speaking to them, I mean. Would he approve of that? I know how very particular nice Americans are. I think your action might make a difference; it would certainly carry weight with Lady Susan."

"Dear Miss Pinsent, you flatter me!"

Lydia rose and gathered up her book and sunshade.

"Well, if you're asked for an opinion, if Lady Susan asks you for one, I think you ought to be prepared," Miss Pinsent admonished her as she moved away.

III

Lady Susan held her own. She ignored the Lintons, and her little family, as Miss Pinsent phrased it, followed suit. Even Mrs. Ainger agreed that it was obligatory. If Lady Susan owed it to the others not to speak to the Lintons, the others clearly owed it to Lady Susan to back her up. It was generally found expedient, at the Hotel Bellosguardo, to adopt this form of reasoning.

Whatever effect this combined action may have had upon the Lintons, it did not at least have that of driving them away. Monsieur Grossart, after a few days of suspense, had the satisfaction of seeing them settle down in his yellow damask premier with what looked like a permanent installation of palm-trees and silk sofa-cushions, and a gratifying continuance in the consumption of champagne. Mrs. Linton trailed her Doucet draperies up and down the garden with the same challenging air, while her husband, smoking innumerable cigarettes, dragged himself dejectedly in her wake; but neither of them, after the first encounter with Lady Susan, made any attempt to extend their acquaintance. They simply ignored their ignorers. As Miss Pinsent resentfully observed, they behaved exactly as though the hotel were empty.

It was therefore a matter of surprise, as well as of displeasure, to Lydia, to find, on glancing up one day from her seat in the garden, that the shadow which had fallen across her book was that of the enigmatic Mrs. Linton.

"I want to speak to you," that lady said, in a rich hard voice that seemed the audible expression of her gown and her complexion.

Lydia started. She certainly did not want to speak to Mrs. Linton.

"Shall I sit down here?" the latter continued, fixing her intensely-shaded eyes on Lydia's face, "or are you afraid of being seen with me?"

"Afraid?" Lydia colored. "Sit down, please. What is it that you wish to say?"

Mrs. Linton, with a smile, drew up a garden-chair and crossed one open- work ankle above the other.

"I want you to tell me what my husband said to your husband last night."

Lydia turned pale.

"My husband—to yours?" she faltered, staring at the other.

"Didn't you know they were closeted together for hours in the smoking-room after you went upstairs? My man didn't get to bed until nearly two o'clock and when he did I couldn't get a word out of him. When he wants to be aggravating I'll back him against anybody living!" Her teeth and eyes flashed persuasively upon Lydia. "But you'll tell me what they were talking about, won't you? I know I can trust you, you look so awfully kind. And it's for his own good. He's such a precious donkey and I'm so afraid he's got into some beastly scrape or other. If he'd only trust his own old woman! But they're always writing to him and setting him against me. And I've got nobody to turn to." She laid her hand on Lydia's with a rattle of bracelets. "You'll help me, won't you?"

Lydia drew back from the smiling fierceness of her brows.

"I'm sorry, but I don't think I understand. My husband has said nothing to me of—of yours."

The great black crescents above Mrs. Linton's eyes met angrily.

"I say—is that true?" she demanded.

Lydia rose from her seat.

"Oh, look here, I didn't mean that, you know, you mustn't take one up so! Can't you see how rattled I am?"

Lydia saw that, in fact, her beautiful mouth was quivering beneath softened eyes.

"I'm beside myself!" the splendid creature wailed, dropping into her seat.

"I'm so sorry," Lydia repeated, forcing herself to speak kindly; "but how can I help you?"

Mrs. Linton raised her head sharply.

"By finding out—there's a darling!"

"Finding what out?"

"What Trevenna told him."

"Trevenna—?" Lydia echoed in bewilderment.

Mrs. Linton clapped her hand to her mouth.

"Oh, Lord—there, it's out! What a fool I am! But I supposed of course you knew; I supposed everybody knew." She dried her eyes and bridled. "Didn't you know that he's Lord Trevenna? I'm Mrs. Cope."

Lydia recognized the names. They had figured in a flamboyant elopement which had thrilled fashionable London some six months earlier.

"Now you see how it is—you understand, don't you?" Mrs. Cope continued on a note of appeal. "I knew you would—that's the reason I came to you. I suppose he felt the same thing about your husband; he's not spoken to another soul in the place." Her face grew anxious again. "He's awfully sensitive, generally, he feels our position, he says, as if it wasn't my place to feel that! But when he does get talking there's no knowing what he'll say. I know he's been brooding over something lately, and I must find out what it is, it's to his interest that I should. I always tell him that I think only of his interest; if he'd only trust me! But he's been so odd lately, I can't think what he's plotting. You will help me, dear?"

Lydia, who had remained standing, looked away uncomfortably.

"If you mean by finding out what Lord Trevenna has told my husband, I'm afraid it's impossible."

"Why impossible?"

"Because I infer that it was told in confidence."

Mrs. Cope stared incredulously.

"Well, what of that? Your husband looks such a dear—anyone can see he's awfully gone on you. What's to prevent your getting it out of him?"

Lydia flushed.

"I'm not a spy!" she exclaimed.

"A spy—a spy? How dare you?" Mrs. Cope flamed out. "Oh, I don't mean that either! Don't be angry with me—I'm so miserable." She essayed a softer note. "Do you call that spying—for one woman to help out another? I do need help so dreadfully! I'm at my wits' end with Trevenna, I am indeed. He's such a boy—a mere baby, you know; he's only two-and-twenty." She dropped her orbed lids. "He's younger than me—only fancy! a few months younger. I tell him he ought to listen to me as if I was his mother; oughtn't he now? But he won't, he won't! All his people are at him, you see—oh, I know their little game! Trying to get him away from me before I can get my divorce—that's what they're up to. At first he wouldn't listen to them; he used to toss their letters over to me to read; but now he reads them himself, and answers 'em too, I fancy; he's always shut up in his room, writing. If I only knew what his plan is I could stop him fast enough—he's such a simpleton. But he's dreadfully deep too—at times I can't make him out. But I know he's told your husband everything—I knew that last night the minute I laid eyes on him. And I must find out, you must help me, I've got no one else to turn to!"

She caught Lydia's fingers in a stormy pressure.

"Say you'll help me, you and your husband."

Lydia tried to free herself.

"What you ask is impossible; you must see that it is. No one could interfere in—in the way you ask."

Mrs. Cope's clutch tightened.

"You won't, then? You won't?"

"Certainly not. Let me go, please."

Mrs. Cope released her with a laugh.

"Oh, go by all means, pray don't let me detain you! Shall you go and tell Lady Susan Condit that there's a pair of us, or shall I save you the trouble of enlightening her?"

Lydia stood still in the middle of the path, seeing her antagonist through a mist of terror. Mrs. Cope was still laughing.

"Oh, I'm not spiteful by nature, my dear; but you're a little more than flesh and blood can stand! It's impossible, is it? Let you go, indeed! You're too good to be mixed up in my affairs, are you? Why, you little fool, the first day I laid eyes on you I saw that you and I were both in the same box, that's the reason I spoke to you."

She stepped nearer, her smile dilating on Lydia like a lamp through a fog.

"You can take your choice, you know; I always play fair. If you'll tell I'll promise not to. Now then, which is it to be?"

Lydia, involuntarily, had begun to move away from the pelting storm of words; but at this she turned and sat down again.

"You may go," she said simply. "I shall stay here."

IV

She stayed there for a long time, in the hypnotized contemplation, not of Mrs. Cope's present, but of her own past. Gannett, early that morning, had gone off on a long walk—he had fallen into the habit of taking these mountain-tramps with various fellow-lodgers; but even had he been within reach she could not have gone to him just then. She had to deal with herself first. She was surprised to find how, in the last months, she had lost the habit of introspection. Since their coming to the Hotel Bellosguardo she and Gannett had tacitly avoided themselves and each other.

She was aroused by the whistle of the three o'clock steamboat as it neared the landing just beyond the hotel gates. Three o'clock! Then Gannett would soon be back, he had told her to expect him before four. She rose hurriedly, her face averted from the inquisitorial facade of the hotel. She could not see him just yet; she could not go indoors. She slipped through one of the overgrown garden-alleys and climbed a steep path to the hills.

It was dark when she opened their sitting-room door. Gannett was sitting on the window-ledge smoking a cigarette. Cigarettes were now his chief resource: he had not written a line during the two months they had spent at the Hotel Bellosguardo. In that respect, it had turned out not to be the right milieu after all.

He started up at Lydia's entrance.

"Where have you been? I was getting anxious."

She sat down in a chair near the door.

"Up the mountain," she said wearily.

"Alone?"

"Yes."

Gannett threw away his cigarette: the sound of her voice made him want to see her face.

"Shall we have a little light?" he suggested.

She made no answer and he lifted the globe from the lamp and put a match to the wick. Then he looked at her.

"Anything wrong? You look done up."

She sat glancing vaguely about the little sitting-room, dimly lit by the pallid-globed lamp, which left in twilight the outlines of the furniture, of his writing-table heaped with books and papers, of the tea-roses and jasmine drooping on the mantel-piece. How like home it had all grown, how like home!

"Lydia, what is wrong?" he repeated.

She moved away from him, feeling for her hatpins and turning to lay her hat and sunshade on the table.

Suddenly she said: "That woman has been talking to me."

Gannett stared.

"That woman? What woman?"

"Mrs. Linton—Mrs. Cope."

He gave a start of annoyance, still, as she perceived, not grasping the full import of her words.

"The deuce! She told you—?"

"She told me everything."

Gannett looked at her anxiously.

"What impudence! I'm so sorry that you should have been exposed to this, dear."

"Exposed!" Lydia laughed.

Gannett's brow clouded and they looked away from each other.

"Do you know why she told me? She had the best of reasons. The first time she laid eyes on me she saw that we were both in the same box."

"Lydia!"

"So it was natural, of course, that she should turn to me in a difficulty."

"What difficulty?"

"It seems she has reason to think that Lord Trevenna's people are trying to get him away from her before she gets her divorce—"

"Well?"

"And she fancied he had been consulting with you last night as to—as to the best way of escaping from her."

Gannett stood up with an angry forehead.

"Well—what concern of yours was all this dirty business? Why should she go to you?"

"Don't you see? It's so simple. I was to wheedle his secret out of you."

"To oblige that woman?"

"Yes; or, if I was unwilling to oblige her, then to protect myself."

"To protect yourself? Against whom?"

"Against her telling everyone in the hotel that she and I are in the same box."

"She threatened that?"

"She left me the choice of telling it myself or of doing it for me."

"The beast!"

There was a long silence. Lydia had seated herself on the sofa, beyond the radius of the lamp, and he leaned against the window. His next question surprised her.

"When did this happen? At what time, I mean?" She looked at him vaguely.

"I don't know—after luncheon, I think. Yes, I remember; it must have been at about three o'clock."

He stepped into the middle of the room and as he approached the light she saw that his brow had cleared.

"Why do you ask?" she said.

"Because when I came in, at about half-past three, the mail was just being distributed, and Mrs. Cope was waiting as usual to pounce on her letters; you know she was always watching for the postman. She was standing so close to me that I couldn't help seeing a big official-looking envelope that was handed to her. She tore it open, gave one look at the inside, and rushed off upstairs like a whirlwind, with the director shouting after her that she had left all her other letters behind. I don't believe she ever thought of you again after that paper was put into her hand."

"Why?"

"Because she was too busy. I was sitting in the window, watching for you, when the five o'clock boat left, and who should go on board, bag and baggage, valet and maid, dressing-bags and poodle, but Mrs. Cope and Trevenna. Just an hour and a half to pack up in! And you should have seen her when they started. She was radiant, shaking hands with everybody, waving her handkerchief from the deck—distributing bows and smiles like an empress. If ever a woman got what she wanted just in the nick of time that woman did. She'll be Lady Trevenna within a week, I'll wager."

"You think she has her divorce?"

"I'm sure of it. And she must have got it just after her talk with you."

Lydia was silent.

At length she said, with a kind of reluctance, "She was horribly angry when she left me. It wouldn't have taken long to tell Lady Susan Condit."

"Lady Susan Condit has not been told."

"How do you know?"

"Because when I went downstairs half an hour ago I met Lady Susan on the way—"

He stopped, half smiling.

"Well?"

"And she stopped to ask if I thought you would act as patroness to a charity concert she is getting up."

In spite of themselves they both broke into a laugh. Lydia's ended in sobs and she sank down with her face hidden. Gannett bent over her, seeking her hands.

"That vile woman—I ought to have warned you to keep away from her; I can't forgive myself! But he spoke to me in confidence; and I never dreamed—well, it's all over now."

Lydia lifted her head.

"Not for me. It's only just beginning."

"What do you mean?"

She put him gently aside and moved in her turn to the window. Then she went on, with her face turned toward the shimmering blackness of the lake, "You see of course that it might happen again at any moment."

"What?"

"This—this risk of being found out. And we could hardly count again on such a lucky combination of chances, could we?"

He sat down with a groan.

Still keeping her face toward the darkness, she said, "I want you to go and tell Lady Susan—and the others."

Gannett, who had moved towards her, paused a few feet off.

"Why do you wish me to do this?" he said at length, with less surprise in his voice than she had been prepared for.

"Because I've behaved basely, abominably, since we came here: letting these people believe we were married—lying with every breath I drew—"

"Yes, I've felt that too," Gannett exclaimed with sudden energy.

The words shook her like a tempest: all her thoughts seemed to fall about her in ruins.

"You—you've felt so?"

"Of course I have." He spoke with low-voiced vehemence. "Do you suppose I like playing the sneak any better than you do? It's damnable."

He had dropped on the arm of a chair, and they stared at each other like blind people who suddenly see.

"But you have liked it here," she faltered.

"Oh, I've liked it, I've liked it." He moved impatiently. "Haven't you?"

"Yes," she burst out; "that's the worst of it, that's what I can't bear. I fancied it was for your sake that I insisted on staying, because you thought you could write here; and perhaps just at first that really was the reason. But afterwards I wanted to stay myself, I loved it." She broke into a laugh. "Oh, do you see the full derision of it? These people, the very prototypes of the bores you took me away from, with the same fenced, in view of life, the same keep-off-the-grass morality, the same little cautious virtues and the same little frightened vices—well, I've clung to them, I've delighted in them, I've done my best to please them. I've toadied Lady Susan, I've gossiped with Miss Pinsent, I've pretended to be shocked with Mrs. Ainger. Respectability! It was the one thing in life that I was sure I didn't care about, and it's grown so precious to me that I've stolen it because I couldn't get it in any other way."

She moved across the room and returned to his side with another laugh.

"I who used to fancy myself unconventional! I must have been born with a card-case in my hand. You should have seen me with that poor woman in the garden. She came to me for help, poor creature, because she fancied that, having 'sinned,' as they call it, I might feel some pity for others who had been tempted in the same way. Not I! She didn't know me. Lady Susan would have been kinder, because Lady Susan wouldn't have been afraid. I hated the woman—my one thought was not to be seen with her—I could have killed her for guessing my secret. The one thing that mattered to me at that moment was my standing with Lady Susan!"

Gannett did not speak.

"And you—you've felt it too!" she broke out accusingly. "You've enjoyed being with these people as much as I have; you've let the chaplain talk to you by the hour about 'The Reign of Law' and Professor Drummond. When they asked you to hand the plate in church I was watching you—you wanted to accept."

She stepped close, laying her hand on his arm.

"Do you know, I begin to see what marriage is for. It's to keep people away from each other. Sometimes I think that two people who love each other can be saved from madness only by the things that come between them—children, duties, visits, bores, relations—the things that protect married people from each other. We've been too close together—that has been our sin. We've seen the nakedness of each other's souls."

She sank again on the sofa, hiding her face in her hands.

Gannett stood above her perplexedly: he felt as though she were being swept away by some implacable current while he stood helpless on its bank.

At length he said, "Lydia, don't think me a brute—but don't you see yourself that it won't do?"

"Yes, I see it won't do," she said without raising her head.

His face cleared.

"Then we'll go to-morrow."

"Go—where?"

"To Paris; to be married."

For a long time she made no answer; then she asked slowly, "Would they have us here if we were married?"

"Have us here?"

"I mean Lady Susan—and the others."

"Have us here? Of course they would."

"Not if they knew, at least, not unless they could pretend not to know."

He made an impatient gesture.

"We shouldn't come back here, of course; and other people needn't know, no one need know."

She sighed. "Then it's only another form of deception and a meaner one. Don't you see that?"

"I see that we're not accountable to any Lady Susans on earth!"

"Then why are you ashamed of what we are doing here?"

"Because I'm sick of pretending that you're my wife when you're not—when you won't be."

She looked at him sadly.

"If I were your wife you'd have to go on pretending. You'd have to pretend that I'd never been—anything else. And our friends would have to pretend that they believed what you pretended."

Gannett pulled off the sofa-tassel and flung it away.

"You're impossible," he groaned.

"It's not I—it's our being together that's impossible. I only want you to see that marriage won't help it."

"What will help it then?"

She raised her head.

"My leaving you."

"Your leaving me?" He sat motionless, staring at the tassel which lay at the other end of the room. At length some impulse of retaliation for the pain she was inflicting made him say deliberately:

"And where would you go if you left me?"

"Oh!" she cried.

He was at her side in an instant.

"Lydia—Lydia—you know I didn't mean it; I couldn't mean it! But you've driven me out of my senses; I don't know what I'm saying. Can't you get out of this labyrinth of self-torture? It's destroying us both."

"That's why I must leave you."

"How easily you say it!" He drew her hands down and made her face him. "You're very scrupulous about yourself—and others. But have you thought of me? You have no right to leave me unless you've ceased to care—"

"It's because I care—"

"Then I have a right to be heard. If you love me you can't leave me."

Her eyes defied him.

"Why not?"

He dropped her hands and rose from her side.

"Can you?" he said sadly.

The hour was late and the lamp flickered and sank. She stood up with a shiver and turned toward the door of her room.

V

At daylight a sound in Lydia's room woke Gannett from a troubled sleep. He sat up and listened. She was moving about softly, as though fearful of disturbing him. He heard her push back one of the creaking shutters; then there was a moment's silence, which seemed to indicate that she was waiting to see if the noise had roused him.

Presently she began to move again. She had spent a sleepless night, probably, and was dressing to go down to the garden for a breath of air. Gannett rose also; but some undefinable instinct made his movements as cautious as hers. He stole to his window and looked out through the slats of the shutter.

It had rained in the night and the dawn was gray and lifeless. The cloud- muffled hills across the lake were reflected in its surface as in a tarnished mirror. In the garden, the birds were beginning to shake the drops from the motionless laurustinus-boughs.

An immense pity for Lydia filled Gannett's soul. Her seeming intellectual independence had blinded him for a time to the feminine cast of her mind. He had never thought of her as a woman who wept and clung: there was a lucidity in her intuitions that made them appear to be the result of reasoning. Now he saw the cruelty he had committed in detaching her from the normal conditions of life; he felt, too, the insight with which she had hit upon the real cause of their suffering. Their life was "impossible," as she had said, and its worst penalty was that it had made any other life impossible for them. Even had his love lessened, he was bound to her now by a hundred ties of pity and self-reproach; and she, poor child! must turn back to him as Latude returned to his cell....

A new sound startled him: it was the stealthy closing of Lydia's door. He crept to his own and heard her footsteps passing down the corridor. Then he went back to the window and looked out.

A minute or two later he saw her go down the steps of the porch and enter the garden. From his post of observation her face was invisible, but something about her appearance struck him. She wore a long travelling cloak and under its folds he detected the outline of a bag or bundle. He drew a deep breath and stood watching her.

She walked quickly down the laurustinus alley toward the gate; there she paused a moment, glancing about the little shady square. The stone benches under the trees were empty, and she seemed to gather resolution from the solitude about her, for she crossed the square to the steam-boat landing, and he saw her pause before the ticket-office at the head of the wharf. Now she was buying her ticket. Gannett turned his head a moment to look at the clock: the boat was due in five minutes. He had time to jump into his clothes and overtake her—

He made no attempt to move; an obscure reluctance restrained him. If any thought emerged from the tumult of his sensations, it was that he must let her go if she wished it. He had spoken last night of his rights: what were they? At the last issue, he and she were two separate beings, not made one by the miracle of common forbearances, duties, abnegations, but bound together in a noyade of passion that left them resisting yet clinging as they went down.

After buying her ticket, Lydia had stood for a moment looking out across the lake; then he saw her seat herself on one of the benches near the landing. He and she, at that moment, were both listening for the same sound: the whistle of the boat as it rounded the nearest promontory. Gannett turned again to glance at the clock: the boat was due now.

Where would she go? What would her life be when she had left him? She had no near relations and few friends. There was money enough ... but she asked so much of life, in ways so complex and immaterial. He thought of her as walking bare-footed through a stony waste. No one would understand her, no one would pity her, and he, who did both, was powerless to come to her aid....

He saw that she had risen from the bench and walked toward the edge of the lake. She stood looking in the direction from which the steamboat was to come; then she turned to the ticket-office, doubtless to ask the cause of the delay. After that she went back to the bench and sat down with bent head. What was she thinking of?

The whistle sounded; she started up, and Gannett involuntarily made a movement toward the door. But he turned back and continued to watch her. She stood motionless, her eyes on the trail of smoke that preceded the appearance of the boat. Then the little craft rounded the point, a dead-white object on the leaden water: a minute later it was puffing and backing at the wharf.

The few passengers who were waiting, two or three peasants and a snuffy priest, were clustered near the ticket-office. Lydia stood apart under the trees.

The boat lay alongside now; the gang-plank was run out and the peasants went on board with their baskets of vegetables, followed by the priest. Still Lydia did not move. A bell began to ring querulously; there was a shriek of steam, and someone must have called to her that she would be late, for she started forward, as though in answer to a summons. She moved waveringly, and at the edge of the wharf she paused. Gannett saw a sailor beckon to her; the bell rang again and she stepped upon the gang-plank.

Half-way down the short incline to the deck she stopped again; then she turned and ran back to the land. The gang-plank was drawn in, the bell ceased to ring, and the boat backed out into the lake. Lydia, with slow steps, was walking toward the garden....

As she approached the hotel she looked up furtively and Gannett drew back into the room. He sat down beside a table; a Bradshaw lay at his elbow, and mechanically, without knowing what he did, he began looking out the trains to Paris....

A COWARD

"My daughter Irene," said Mrs. Carstyle (she made it rhyme with tureen), "has had no social advantages; but if Mr. Carstyle had chosen—" she paused significantly and looked at the shabby sofa on the opposite side of the fire-place as though it had been Mr. Carstyle. Vibart was glad that it was not.

Mrs. Carstyle was one of the women who make refinement vulgar. She invariably spoke of her husband as Mr. Carstyle and, though she had but one daughter, was always careful to designate the young lady by name. At luncheon she had talked a great deal of elevating influences and ideals, and had fluctuated between apologies for the overdone mutton and affected surprise that the bewildered maid-servant should have forgotten to serve the coffee and liqueurs as usual.

Vibart was almost sorry that he had come. Miss Carstyle was still beautiful, almost as beautiful as when, two days earlier, against the leafy background of a June garden-party, he had seen her for the first time, but her mother's expositions and elucidations cheapened her beauty as sign-posts vulgarize a woodland solitude. Mrs. Carstyle's eye was perpetually plying between her daughter and Vibart, like an empty cab in quest of a fare. Miss Carstyle, the young man decided, was the kind of girl whose surroundings rub off on her; or was it rather that Mrs. Carstyle's idiosyncrasies were of a nature to color every one within reach? Vibart, looking across the table as this consolatory alternative occurred to him, was sure that they had not colored Mr. Carstyle; but that, perhaps, was only because they had bleached him instead. Mr. Carstyle was quite colorless; it would have been impossible to guess his native tint. His wife's qualities, if they had affected him at all, had acted negatively. He did not apologize for the mutton, and he wandered off after luncheon without pretending to wait for the diurnal coffee and liqueurs; while the few remarks that he had contributed to the conversation during the meal had not been in the direction of abstract conceptions of life. As he strayed away, with his vague oblique step, and the stoop that suggested the habit of dodging missiles, Vibart, who was still in the age of formulas, found himself wondering what life could be worth to a man who had evidently resigned himself to travelling with his back to the wind; so that Mrs. Carstyle's allusion to her daughter's lack of advantages (imparted while Irene searched the house for an undiscoverable cigarette) had an appositeness unintended by the speaker.

"If Mr. Carstyle had chosen," that lady repeated, "we might have had our city home" (she never used so small a word as town) "and Ireen could have mixed in the society to which I myself was accustomed at her age." Her sigh pointed unmistakably to a past when young men had come to luncheon to see her.

The sigh led Vibart to look at her, and the look led him to the unwelcome conclusion that Irene "took after" her mother. It was certainly not from the sapless paternal stock that the girl had drawn her warm bloom: Mrs. Carstyle had contributed the high lights to the picture.

Mrs. Carstyle caught his look and appropriated it with the complacency of a vicarious beauty. She was quite aware of the value of her appearance as guaranteeing Irene's development into a fine woman.

"But perhaps," she continued, taking up the thread of her explanation, "you have heard of Mr. Carstyle's extraordinary hallucination. Mr. Carstyle knows that I call it so, as I tell him, it is the most charitable view to take." She looked coldly at the threadbare sofa and indulgently at the young man who filled a corner of it.

"You may think it odd, Mr. Vibart, that I should take you into my confidence in this way after so short an acquaintance, but somehow I can't help regarding you as a friend already. I believe in those intuitive sympathies, don't you? They have never misled me—" her lids drooped retrospectively—"and besides, I always tell Mr. Carstyle that on this point I will have no false pretences. Where truth is concerned I am inexorable, and I consider it my duty to let our friends know that our restricted way of living is due entirely to choice—to Mr. Carstyle's choice. When I married Mr. Carstyle it was with the expectation of living in New York and of keeping my carriage; and there is no reason for our not doing so, there is no reason, Mr. Vibart, why my daughter Ireen should have been denied the intellectual advantages of foreign travel. I wish that to be understood. It is owing to her father's deliberate choice that Ireen and I have been imprisoned in the narrow limits of Millbrook society. For myself I do not complain. If Mr. Carstyle chooses to place others before his wife it is not for his wife to repine. His course may be noble—Quixotic; I do not allow myself to pronounce judgment on it, though others have thought that in sacrificing his own family to strangers he was violating the most sacred obligations of domestic life. This is the opinion of my pastor and of other valued friends; but, as I have always told them, for myself I make no claims. Where my daughter Ireen is concerned it is different—"

It was a relief to Vibart when, at this point, Mrs. Carstyle's discharge of her duty was cut short by her daughter's reappearance. Irene had been unable to find a cigarette for Mr. Vibart, and her mother, with beaming irrelevance, suggested that in that case she had better show him the garden.

The Carstyle house stood but a few yards back from the brick-paved Millbrook street, and the garden was a very small place, unless measured, as Mrs. Carstyle probably intended that it should be, by the extent of her daughter's charms. These were so considerable that Vibart walked back and forward half a dozen times between the porch and the gate, before he discovered the limitations of the Carstyle domain. It was not till Irene had accused him of being sarcastic and had confided in him that "the girls" were furious with her for letting him talk to her so long at his aunt's garden-party, that he awoke to the exiguity of his surroundings; and then it was with a touch of irritation that he noticed Mr. Carstyle's inconspicuous profile bent above a newspaper in one of the lower windows. Vibart had an idea that Mr. Carstyle, while ostensibly reading the paper, had kept count of the number of times that his daughter had led her companion up and down between the syringa-bushes; and for some undefinable reason he resented Mr. Carstyle's unperturbed observation more than his wife's zealous self-effacement. To a man who is trying to please a pretty girl there are moments when the proximity of an impartial spectator is more disconcerting than the most obvious connivance; and something about Mr. Carstyle's expression conveyed his good-humored indifference to Irene's processes.

When the garden-gate closed behind Vibart he had become aware that his preoccupation with the Carstyles had shifted its centre from the daughter to the father; but he was accustomed to such emotional surprises, and skilled in seizing any compensations they might offer.

II

The Carstyles belonged to the all-the-year-round Millbrook of paper-mills, cable-cars, brick pavements and church sociables, while Mrs. Vance, the aunt with whom Vibart lived, was an ornament of the summer colony whose big country-houses dotted the surrounding hills. Mrs. Vance had, however, no difficulty in appeasing the curiosity which Mrs. Carstyle's enigmatic utterances had aroused in the young man. Mrs. Carstyle's relentless veracity vented itself mainly on the "summer people," as they were called: she did not propose that any one within ten miles of Millbrook should keep a carriage without knowing that she was entitled to keep one too. Mrs. Vance remarked with a sigh that Mrs. Carstyle's annual demand to have her position understood came in as punctually as the taxes and the water- rates.

"My dear, it's simply this: when Andrew Carstyle married her years ago—Heaven knows why he did; he's one of the Albany Carstyles, you know, and she was a daughter of old Deacon Ash of South Millbrook—well, when he married her he had a tidy little income, and I suppose the bride expected to set up an establishment in New York and be hand-in-glove with the whole Carstyle clan. But whether he was ashamed of her from the first, or for some other unexplained reason, he bought a country-place and settled down here for life. For a few years they lived comfortably enough, and she had plenty of smart clothes, and drove about in a victoria calling on the summer people. Then, when the beautiful Irene was about ten years old, Mr. Carstyle's only brother died, and it turned out that he had made away with a lot of trust-property. It was a horrid business: over three hundred thousand dollars were gone, and of course most of it had belonged to widows and orphans. As soon as the facts were made known, Andrew Carstyle announced that he would pay back what his brother had stolen. He sold his country-place and his wife's carriage, and they moved to the little house they live in now. Mr. Carstyle's income is probably not as large as his wife would like to have it thought, and though I'm told he puts aside, a good part of it every year to pay off his brother's obligations, I fancy the debt won't be discharged for some time to come. To help things along he opened a law office, he had studied law in his youth, but though he is said to be clever I hear that he has very little to do. People are afraid of him: he's too dry and quiet. Nobody believes in a man who doesn't believe in himself, and Mr. Carstyle always seems to be winking at you through a slit in his professional manner. People don't like it, his wife doesn't like it. I believe she would have accepted the sacrifice of the country-place and the carriage if he had struck an attitude and talked about doing his duty. It was his regarding the whole thing as a matter of course that exasperated her. What is the use of doing something difficult in a way that makes it look perfectly easy? I feel sorry for Mrs. Carstyle. She's lost her house and her carriage, and she hasn't been allowed to be heroic."

Vibart had listened attentively.

"I wonder what Miss Carstyle thinks of it?" he mused.

Mrs. Vance looked at him with a tentative smile. "I wonder what you think of Miss Carstyle?" she returned,

His answer reassured her.

"I think she takes after her mother," he said.

"Ah," cried his aunt cheerfully, "then I needn't write to your mother, and I can have Irene at all my parties!"

Miss Carstyle was an important factor in the restricted social combinations of a Millbrook hostess. A local beauty is always a useful addition to a Saturday-to-Monday house-party, and the beautiful Irene was served up as a perennial novelty to the jaded guests of the summer colony. As Vibart's aunt remarked, she was perfect till she became playful, and she never became playful till the third day.

Under these conditions, it was natural that Vibart should see a good deal of the young lady, and before he was aware of it he had drifted into the anomalous position of paying court to the daughter in order to ingratiate himself with the father. Miss Carstyle was beautiful, Vibart was young, and the days were long in his aunt's spacious and distinguished house; but it was really the desire to know something more of Mr. Carstyle that led the young man to partake so often of that gentleman's overdone mutton. Vibart's imagination had been touched by the discovery that this little huddled-up man, instead of travelling with the wind, was persistently facing a domestic gale of considerable velocity. That he should have paid off his brother's debt at one stroke was to the young man a conceivable feat; but that he should go on methodically and uninterruptedly accumulating the needed amount, under the perpetual accusation of Irene's inadequate frocks and Mrs. Carstyle's apologies for the mutton, seemed to Vibart proof of unexampled heroism. Mr. Carstyle was as inaccessible as the average American parent, and led a life so detached from the preoccupations of his womankind that Vibart had some difficulty in fixing his attention. To Mr. Carstyle, Vibart was simply the inevitable young man who had been hanging about the house ever since Irene had left school; and Vibart's efforts to differentiate himself from this enamored abstraction were hampered by Mrs. Carstyle's cheerful assumption that he was the young man, and by Irene's frank appropriation of his visits.

In this extremity he suddenly observed a slight but significant change in the manner of the two ladies. Irene, instead of charging him with being sarcastic and horrid, and declaring herself unable to believe a word he said, began to receive his remarks with the impersonal smile which he had seen her accord to the married men of his aunt's house-parties; while Mrs. Carstyle, talking over his head to an invisible but evidently sympathetic and intelligent listener, debated the propriety of Irene's accepting an invitation to spend the month of August at Narragansett. When Vibart, rashly trespassing on the rights of this unseen oracle, remarked that a few weeks at the seashore would make a delightful change for Miss Carstyle, the ladies looked at him and then laughed.

It was at this point that Vibart, for the first time, found himself observed by Mr. Carstyle. They were grouped about the debris of a luncheon which had ended precipitously with veal stew (Mrs. Carstyle explaining that poor cooks always failed with their sweet dish when there was company) and Mr. Carstyle, his hands thrust in his pockets, his lean baggy-coated shoulders pressed against his chair-back, sat contemplating his guest with a smile of unmistakable approval. When Vibart caught his eye the smile vanished, and Mr. Carstyle, dropping his glasses from the bridge of his thin nose, looked out of the window with the expression of a man determined to prove an alibi. But Vibart was sure of the smile: it had established, between his host and himself, a complicity which Mr. Carstyle's attempted evasion served only to confirm.

On the strength of this incident Vibart, a few days later, called at Mr. Carstyle's office. Ostensibly, the young man had come to ask, on his aunt's behalf, some question on a point at issue between herself and the Millbrook telephone company; but his purpose in offering to perform the errand had been the hope of taking up his intercourse with Mr. Carstyle where that gentleman's smile had left it. Vibart was not disappointed. In a dingy office, with a single window looking out on a blank wall, he found Mr. Carstyle, in an alpaca coat, reading Montaigne.

It evidently did not occur to him that Vibart had come on business, and the warmth of his welcome gave the young man a sense of furnishing the last word in a conjugal argument in which, for once, Mr. Carstyle had come off triumphant.

The legal question disposed of, Vibart reverted to Montaigne: had Mr. Carstyle seen young So-and-so's volume of essays? There was one on Montaigne that had a decided flavor: the point of view was curious. Vibart was surprised to find that Mr. Carstyle had heard of young So-and-so. Clever young men are given to thinking that their elders have never got beyond Macaulay; but Mr. Carstyle seemed sufficiently familiar with recent literature not to take it too seriously. He accepted Vibart's offer of young So-and-so's volume, admitting that his own library was not exactly up-to-date.

Vibart went away musing. The next day he came back with the volume of essays. It seemed to be tacitly understood that he was to call at the office when he wished to see Mr. Carstyle, whose legal engagements did not seriously interfere with the pursuit of literature.

For a week or ten days Mrs. Carstyle, in Vibart's presence, continued to take counsel with her unseen adviser on the subject of her daughter's visit to Narragansett. Once or twice Irene dropped her impersonal smile to tax Vibart with not caring whether she went or not; and Mrs. Carstyle seized a moment of tete-a-tete to confide in him that the dear child hated the idea of leaving, and was going only because her friend Mrs. Higby would not let her off. Of course, if it had not been for Mr. Carstyle's peculiarities they would have had their own seaside home—at Newport, probably: Mrs. Carstyle preferred the tone of Newport—and Irene would not have been dependent on the charity of her friends; but as it was, they must be thankful for small mercies, and Mrs. Higby was certainly very kind in her way, and had a charming social position—for Narragansett.

These confidences, however, were soon superseded by an exchange, between mother and daughter, of increasingly frequent allusions to the delights of Narragansett, the popularity of Mrs. Higby, and the jolliness of her house; with an occasional reference on Mrs. Carstyle's part to the probability of Hewlett Bain's being there as usual—hadn't Irene heard from Mrs. Higby that he was to be there? Upon this note Miss Carstyle at length departed, leaving Vibart to the undisputed enjoyment of her father's company.

Vibart had at no time a keen taste for the summer joys of Millbrook, and the family obligation which, for several months of the year, kept him at his aunt's side (Mrs. Vance was a childless widow and he filled the onerous post of favorite nephew) gave a sense of compulsion to the light occupations that chequered his leisure. Mrs. Vance, who fancied herself lonely when he was away, was too much engaged with notes, telegrams and arriving and departing guests, to do more than breathlessly smile upon his presence, or implore him to take the dullest girl of the party for a drive (and would he go by way of Millbrook, like a dear, and stop at the market to ask why the lobsters hadn't come?); and the house itself, and the guests who came and went in it like people rushing through a railway- station, offered no points of repose to his thoughts. Some houses are companions in themselves: the walls, the book-shelves, the very chairs and tables, have the qualities of a sympathetic mind; but Mrs. Vance's interior was as impersonal as the setting of a classic drama.

These conditions made Vibart cultivate an assiduous exchange of books between himself and Mr. Carstyle. The young man went down almost daily to the little house in the town, where Mrs. Carstyle, who had now an air of receiving him in curl-papers, and of not always immediately distinguishing him from the piano-tuner, made no effort to detain him on his way to her husband's study.

III

Now and then, at the close of one of Vibart's visits, Mr. Carstyle put on a mildewed Panama hat and accompanied the young man for a mile or two on his way home. The road to Mrs. Vance's lay through one of the most amiable suburbs of Millbrook, and Mr. Carstyle, walking with his slow uneager step, his hat pushed back, and his stick dragging behind him, seemed to take a philosophic pleasure in the aspect of the trim lawns and opulent gardens.

Vibart could never induce his companion to prolong his walk as far as Mrs. Vance's drawing-room; but one afternoon, when the distant hills lay blue beyond the twilight of overarching elms, the two men strolled on into the country past that lady's hospitable gateposts.

It was a still day, the road was deserted, and every sound came sharply through the air. Mr. Carstyle was in the midst of a disquisition on Diderot, when he raised his head and stood still.

"What's that?" he said. "Listen!"

Vibart listened and heard a distant storm of hoof-beats. A moment later, a buggy drawn by a pair of trotters swung round the turn of the road. It was about thirty yards off, coming toward them at full speed. The man who drove was leaning forward with outstretched arms; beside him sat a girl.

Suddenly Vibart saw Mr. Carstyle jump into the middle of the road, in front of the buggy. He stood there immovable, his arms extended, his legs apart, in an attitude of indomitable resistance. Almost at the same moment Vibart realized that the man in the buggy had his horses in hand.

"They're not running!" Vibart shouted, springing into the road and catching Mr. Carstyle's alpaca sleeve. The older man looked around vaguely: he seemed dazed.

"Come away, sir, come away!" cried Vibart, gripping his arm. The buggy swept past them, and Mr. Carstyle stood in the dust gazing after it.

At length he drew out his handkerchief and wiped his forehead. He was very pale and Vibart noticed that his hand shook.

"That was a close call, sir, wasn't it? I suppose you thought they were running."

"Yes," said Mr. Carstyle slowly, "I thought they were running."

"It certainly looked like it for a minute. Let's sit down, shall we? I feel rather breathless myself."

Vibart saw that his friend could hardly stand. They seated themselves on a tree-trunk by the roadside, and Mr. Carstyle continued to wipe his forehead in silence.

At length he turned to Vibart and said abruptly:

"I made straight for the middle of the road, didn't I? If there had been a runaway I should have stopped it?"

Vibart looked at him in surprise.

"You would have tried to, undoubtedly, unless I'd had time to drag you away."

Mr. Carstyle straightened his narrow shoulders.

"There was no hesitation, at all events? I—I showed no signs of—avoiding it?"

"I should say not, sir; it was I who funked it for you."

Mr. Carstyle was silent: his head had dropped forward and he looked like an old man.

"It was just my cursed luck again!" he exclaimed suddenly in a loud voice.

For a moment Vibart thought that he was wandering; but he raised his head and went on speaking in more natural tones.

"I daresay I appeared ridiculous enough to you just now, eh? Perhaps you saw all along that the horses weren't running? Your eyes are younger than mine; and then you're not always looking out for runaways, as I am. Do you know that in thirty years I've never seen a runaway?"

"You're fortunate," said Vibart, still bewildered.

"Fortunate? Good God, man, I've prayed to see one: not a runaway especially, but any bad accident; anything that endangered people's lives. There are accidents happening all the time all over the world; why shouldn't I ever come across one? It's not for want of trying! At one time I used to haunt the theatres in the hope of a fire: fires in theatres are so apt to be fatal. Well, will you believe it? I was in the Brooklyn theatre the night before it burned down; I left the old Madison Square Garden half an hour before the walls fell in. And it's the same way with street accidents—I always miss them; I'm always just too late. Last year there was a boy knocked down by a cable-car at our corner; I got to my gate just as they were carrying him off on a stretcher. And so it goes. If anybody else had been walking along this road, those horses would have been running away. And there was a girl in the buggy, too—a mere child!"

Mr. Carstyle's head sank again.

"You're wondering what this means," he began after another pause. "I was a little confused for a moment—must have seemed incoherent." His voice cleared and he made an effort to straighten himself. "Well, I was a damned coward once and I've been trying to live it down ever since."

Vibart looked at him incredulously and Mr. Carstyle caught the look with a smile.

"Why not? Do I look like a Hercules?" He held up his loose-skinned hand and shrunken wrist. "Not built for the part, certainly; but that doesn't count, of course. Man's unconquerable soul, and all the rest of it ... well, I was a coward every inch of me, body and soul."

He paused and glanced up and down the road. There was no one in sight.

"It happened when I was a young chap just out of college. I was travelling round the world with another youngster of my own age and an older man, Charles Meriton, who has since made a name for himself. You may have heard of him."

"Meriton, the archaeologist? The man who discovered those ruined African cities the other day?"

"That's the man. He was a college tutor then, and my father, who had known him since he was a boy, and who had a very high opinion of him, had asked him to make the tour with us. We both, my friend Collis and I, had an immense admiration for Meriton. He was just the fellow to excite a boy's enthusiasm: cool, quick, imperturbable, the kind of man whose hand is always on the hilt of action. His explorations had led him into all sorts of tight places, and he'd shown an extraordinary combination of calculating patience and reckless courage. He never talked about his doings; we picked them up from various people on our journey. He'd been everywhere, he knew everybody, and everybody had something stirring to tell about him. I daresay this account of the man sounds exaggerated; perhaps it is; I've never seen him since; but at that time he seemed to me a tremendous fellow, a kind of scientific Ajax. He was a capital travelling-companion, at any rate: good-tempered, cheerful, easily amused, with none of the been-there-before superiority so irritating to youngsters. He made us feel as though it were all as new to him as to us: he never chilled our enthusiasms or took the bloom off our surprises. There was nobody else whose good opinion I cared as much about: he was the biggest thing in sight.

"On the way home Collis broke down with diphtheria. We were in the Mediterranean, cruising about the Sporades in a felucca. He was taken ill at Chios. The attack came on suddenly and we were afraid to run the risk of taking him back to Athens in the felucca. We established ourselves in the inn at Chios and there the poor fellow lay for weeks. Luckily there was a fairly good doctor on the island and we sent to Athens for a sister to help with the nursing. Poor Collis was desperately bad: the diphtheria was followed by partial paralysis. The doctor assured us that the danger was past; he would gradually regain the use of his limbs; but his recovery would be slow. The sister encouraged us too, she had seen such cases before; and he certainly did improve a shade each day. Meriton and I had taken turns with the sister in nursing him, but after the paralysis had set in there wasn't much to do, and there was nothing to prevent Meriton's leaving us for a day or two. He had received word from some place on the coast of Asia Minor that a remarkable tomb had been discovered somewhere in the interior; he had not been willing to take us there, as the journey was not a particularly safe one; but now that we were tied up at Chios there seemed no reason why he shouldn't go and take a look at the place. The expedition would not take more than three days; Collis was convalescent; the doctor and nurse assured us that there was no cause for uneasiness; and so Meriton started off one evening at sunset. I walked down to the quay with him and saw him rowed off to the felucca. I would have given a good deal to be going with him; the prospect of danger allured me.

"'You'll see that Collis is never left alone, won't you?' he shouted back to me as the boat pulled out into the harbor; I remembered I rather resented the suggestion.

"I walked back to the inn and went to bed: the nurse sat up with Collis at night. The next morning I relieved her at the usual hour. It was a sultry day with a queer coppery-looking sky; the air was stifling. In the middle of the day the nurse came to take my place while I dined; when I went back to Collis's room she said she would go out for a breath of air.

"I sat down by Collis's bed and began to fan him with the fan the sister had been using. The heat made him uneasy and I turned him over in bed, for he was still helpless: the whole of his right side was numb. Presently he fell asleep and I went to the window and sat looking down on the hot deserted square, with a bunch of donkeys and their drivers asleep in the shade of the convent-wall across the way. I remember noticing the blue beads about the donkeys' necks.... Were you ever in an earthquake? No? I'd never been in one either. It's an indescribable sensation ... there's a Day of Judgment feeling in the air. It began with the donkeys waking up and trembling; I noticed that and thought it queer. Then the drivers jumped up, I saw the terror in their faces. Then a roar.... I remember noticing a big black crack in the convent-wall opposite, a zig-zag crack, like a flash of lightning in a wood-cut.... I thought of that, too, at the time; then all the bells in the place began to ring, it made a fearful discord.... I saw people rushing across the square ... the air was full of crashing noises. The floor went down under me in a sickening way and then jumped back and pitched me to the ceiling ... but where was the ceiling? And the door? I said to myself: We're two stories up, the stairs are just wide enough for one.... I gave one glance at Collis: he was lying in bed, wide awake, looking straight at me. I ran. Something struck me on the head as I bolted downstairs, I kept on running. I suppose the knock I got dazed me, for I don't remember much of anything till I found myself in a vineyard a mile from the town. I was roused by the warm blood running down my nose and heard myself explaining to Meriton exactly how it had happened....

"When I crawled back to the town they told me that all the houses near the inn were in ruins and that a dozen people had been killed. Collis was among them, of course. The ceiling had come down on him."

Mr. Carstyle wiped his forehead. Vibart sat looking away from him.

"Two days later Meriton came back. I began to tell him the story, but he interrupted me.

"'There was no one with him at the time, then? You'd left him alone?'

"'No, he wasn't alone.'

"'Who was with him? You said the sister was out.'

"'I was with him.'

"'You were with him?'

"I shall never forget Meriton's look. I believe I had meant to explain, to accuse myself, to shout out my agony of soul; but I saw the uselessness of it. A door had been shut between us. Neither of us spoke another word. He was very kind to me on the way home; he looked after me in a motherly way that was a good deal harder to stand than his open contempt. I saw the man was honestly trying to pity me; but it was no good, he simply couldn't."

Mr. Carstyle rose slowly, with a certain stiffness.

"Shall we turn toward home? Perhaps I'm keeping you."

They walked on a few steps in silence; then he spoke again.

"That business altered my whole life. Of course I oughtn't to have allowed it to—that was another form of cowardice. But I saw myself only with Meriton's eyes, it is one of the worst miseries of youth that one is always trying to be somebody else. I had meant to be a Meriton, I saw I'd better go home and study law....

"It's a childish fancy, a survival of the primitive savage, if you like; but from that hour to this I've hankered day and night for a chance to retrieve myself, to set myself right with the man I meant to be. I want to prove to that man that it was all an accident, an unaccountable deviation from my normal instincts; that having once been a coward doesn't mean that a man's cowardly... and I can't, I can't!"

Mr. Carstyle's tone had passed insensibly from agitation to irony. He had got back to his usual objective stand-point.

"Why, I'm a perfect olive-branch," he concluded, with his dry indulgent laugh; "the very babies stop crying at my approach, I carry a sort of millennium about with me, I'd make my fortune as an agent of the Peace Society. I shall go to the grave leaving that other man unconvinced!"

Vibart walked back with him to Millbrook. On her doorstep they met Mrs. Carstyle, flushed and feathered, with a card-case and dusty boots.

"I don't ask you in," she said plaintively, to Vibart, "because I can't answer for the food this evening. My maid-of-all-work tells me that she's going to a ball, which is more than I've done in years! And besides, it would be cruel to ask you to spend such a hot evening in our stuffy little house, the air is so much cooler at Mrs. Vance's. Remember me to Mrs. Vance, please, and tell her how sorry I am that I can no longer include her in my round of visits. When I had my carriage I saw the people I liked, but now that I have to walk, my social opportunities are more limited. I was not obliged to do my visiting on foot when I was younger, and my doctor tells me that to persons accustomed to a carriage no exercise is more injurious than walking."

She glanced at her husband with a smile of unforgiving sweetness.

"Fortunately," she concluded, "it agrees with Mr. Carstyle."

THE TWILIGHT OF THE GOD

I

A Newport drawing-room. Tapestries, flowers, bric-a-brac. Through the windows, a geranium-edged lawn, the cliffs and the sea. Isabel Warland sits reading. Lucius Warland enters in flannels and a yachting-cap.

Isabel. Back already?

Warland. The wind dropped—it turned into a drifting race. Langham took me off the yacht on his launch. What time is it? Two o'clock? Where's Mrs. Raynor?

Isabel. On her way to New York.

Warland. To New York?

Isabel. Precisely. The boat must be just leaving; she started an hour ago and took Laura with her. In fact I'm alone in the house—that is, until this evening. Some people are coming then.

Warland. But what in the world—

Isabel. Her aunt, Mrs. Griscom, has had a fit. She has them constantly. They're not serious, at least they wouldn't be, if Mrs. Griscom were not so rich, and childless. Naturally, under the circumstances, Marian feels a peculiar sympathy for her; her position is such a sad one; there's positively no one to care whether she lives or dies, except her heirs. Of course they all rush to Newburgh whenever she has a fit. It's hard on Marian, for she lives the farthest away; but she has come to an understanding with the housekeeper, who always telegraphs her first, so that she gets a start of several hours. She will be at Newburgh to-night at ten, and she has calculated that the others can't possibly arrive before midnight.

Warland. You have a delightful way of putting things. I suppose you'd talk of me like that.

Isabel. Oh, no. It's too humiliating to doubt one's husband's disinterestedness.

Warland. I wish I had a rich aunt who had fits.

Isabel. If I were wishing I should choose heart-disease.

Warland. There's no doing anything without money or influence.

Isabel (picking up her book). Have you heard from Washington?

Warland. Yes. That's what I was going to speak of when I asked for Mrs. Raynor. I wanted to bid her good-bye.

Isabel. You're going?

Warland. By the five train. Fagott has just wired me that the Ambassador will be in Washington on Monday. He hasn't named his secretaries yet, but there isn't much hope for me. He has a nephew—

Isabel. They always have. Like the Popes.

Warland. Well, I'm going all the same. You'll explain to Mrs. Raynor if she gets back before I do? Are there to be people at dinner? I don't suppose it matters. You can always pick up an extra man on a Saturday.

Isabel. By the way, that reminds me that Marian left me a list of the people who are arriving this afternoon. My novel is so absorbing that I forgot to look at it. Where can it be? Ah, here—Let me see: the Jack Merringtons, Adelaide Clinton, Ned Lender—all from New York, by seven P.M. train. Lewis Darley to-night, by Fall River boat. John Oberville, from Boston at five P.M. Why, I didn't know—

Warland (excitedly). John Oberville? John Oberville? Here? To-day at five o'clock? Let me see—let me look at the list. Are you sure you're not mistaken? Why, she never said a word! Why the deuce didn't you tell me?

Isabel. I didn't know.

Warland. Oberville—Oberville—!

Isabel. Why, what difference does it make?

Warland. What difference? What difference? Don't look at me as if you didn't understand English! Why, if Oberville's coming—(a pause) Look here, Isabel, didn't you know him very well at one time?

Isabel. Very well—yes.

Warland. I thought so, of course, I remember now; I heard all about it before I met you. Let me see, didn't you and your mother spend a winter in Washington when he was Under-secretary of State?

Isabel. That was before the deluge.

Warland. I remember, it all comes back to me. I used to hear it said that he admired you tremendously; there was a report that you were engaged. Don't you remember? Why, it was in all the papers. By Jove, Isabel, what a match that would have been!

Isabel. You are disinterested!

Warland. Well, I can't help thinking—

Isabel. That I paid you a handsome compliment?

Warland (preoccupied). Eh?—Ah, yes—exactly. What was I saying? Oh—about the report of your engagement. (Playfully.) He was awfully gone on you, wasn't he?

Isabel. It's not for me to diminish your triumph.

Warland. By Jove, I can't think why Mrs. Raynor didn't tell me he was coming. A man like that—one doesn't take him for granted, like the piano- tuner! I wonder I didn't see it in the papers.

Isabel. Is he grown such a great man?

Warland. Oberville? Great? John Oberville? I'll tell you what he is—the power behind the throne, the black Pope, the King-maker and all the rest of it. Don't you read the papers? Of course I'll never get on if you won't interest yourself in politics. And to think you might have married that man!

Isabel. And got you your secretaryship!

Warland. Oberville has them all in the hollow of his hand.

Isabel. Well, you'll see him at five o'clock.

Warland. I don't suppose he's ever heard of me, worse luck! (A silence.) Isabel, look here. I never ask questions, do I? But it was so long ago—and Oberville almost belongs to history, he will one of these days at any rate. Just tell me—did he want to marry you?

Isabel. Since you answer for his immortality (after a pause) I was very much in love with him.

Warland. Then of course he did. (Another pause.) But what in the world—

Isabel (musing). As you say, it was so long ago; I don't see why I shouldn't tell you. There was a married woman who had—what is the correct expression?—made sacrifices for him. There was only one sacrifice she objected to making, and he didn't consider himself free. It sounds rather rococo, doesn't it? It was odd that she died the year after we were married.

Warland. Whew!

Isabel (following her own thoughts). I've never seen him since; it must be ten years ago. I'm certainly thirty-two, and I was just twenty-two then. It's curious to talk of it. I had put it away so carefully. How it smells of camphor! And what an old-fashioned cut it has! (Rising.) Where's the list, Lucius? You wanted to know if there were to be people at dinner tonight—

Warland. Here it is—but never mind. Isabel (silence) Isabel—

Isabel. Well?

Warland. It's odd he never married.

Isabel. The comparison is to my disadvantage. But then I met you.

Warland. Don't be so confoundedly sarcastic. I wonder how he'll feel about seeing you. Oh, I don't mean any sentimental rot, of course... but you're an uncommonly agreeable woman. I daresay he'll be pleased to see you again; you're fifty times more attractive than when I married you.

Isabel. I wish your other investments had appreciated at the same rate. Unfortunately my charms won't pay the butcher.

Warland. Damn the butcher!

Isabel. I happened to mention him because he's just written again; but I might as well have said the baker or the candlestick-maker. The candlestick-maker, I wonder what he is, by the way? He must have more faith in human nature than the others, for I haven't heard from him yet. I wonder if there is a Creditor's Polite Letter-writer which they all consult; their style is so exactly alike. I advise you to pass through New York incognito on your way to Washington; their attentions might be oppressive.

Warland. Confoundedly oppressive. What a dog's life it is! My poor Isabel—

Isabel. Don't pity me. I didn't marry yon for a home.

Warland (after a pause). What did you marry me for, if you cared for Oberville? (Another pause.) Eh?

Isabel, Don't make me regret my confidence.

Warland. I beg your pardon.

Isabel. Oh, it was only a subterfuge to conceal the fact that I have no distinct recollection of my reasons. The fact is, a girl's motives in marrying are like a passport—apt to get mislaid. One is so seldom asked for either. But mine certainly couldn't have been mercenary: I never heard a mother praise you to her daughters.

Warland. No, I never was much of a match.

Isabel. You impugn my judgment.

Warland. If I only had a head for business, now, I might have done something by this time. But I'd sooner break stones in the road.

Isabel. It must be very hard to get an opening in that profession. So many of my friends have aspired to it, and yet I never knew anyone who actually did it.

Warland. If I could only get the secretaryship. How that kind of life would suit you! It's as much for you that I want it—

Isabel. And almost as much for the butcher. Don't belittle the circle of your benevolence. (She walks across the room.) Three o'clock already, and Marian asked me to give orders about the carriages. Let me see, Mr. Oberville is the first arrival; if you'll ring I will send word to the stable. I suppose you'll stay now?

Warland. Stay?

Isabel. Not go to Washington. I thought you spoke as if he could help you.

Warland. He could settle the whole thing in five minutes. The President can't refuse him anything. But he doesn't know me; he may have a candidate of his own. It's a pity you haven't seen him for so long, and yet I don't know; perhaps it's just as well. The others don't arrive till seven? It seems as if—How long is he going to be here? Till to-morrow night, I suppose? I wonder what he's come for. The Merringtons will bore him to death, and Adelaide, of course, will be philandering with Lender. I wonder (a pause) if Darley likes boating. (Rings the bell.)

Isabel. Boating?

Warland. Oh, I was only thinking—Where are the matches? One may smoke here, I suppose? (He looks at his wife.) If I were you I'd put on that black gown of yours to-night—the one with the spangles. It's only that Fred Langham asked me to go over to Narragansett in his launch to-morrow morning, and I was thinking that I might take Darley; I always liked Darley.

Isabel (to the footman who enters). Mrs. Raynor wishes the dog-cart sent to the station at five o'clock to meet Mr. Oberville. Footman. Very good, m'm. Shall I serve tea at the usual time, m'm?

Isabel. Yes. That is, when Mr. Oberville arrives.

Footman (going out). Very good, m'm.

Warland (to Isabel, who is moving toward the door). Where are you going?

Isabel. To my room now—for a walk later.

Warland. Later? It's past three already.

Isabel. I've no engagement this afternoon.

Warland. Oh, I didn't know. (As she reaches the door.) You'll be back, I suppose?

Isabel. I have no intention of eloping.

Warland. For tea, I mean?

Isabel. I never take tea. (Warland shrugs his shoulders.)

The same drawing-room. Isabel enters from the lawn in hat and gloves. The tea-table is set out, and the footman just lighting the lamp under the kettle.

Isabel. You may take the tea-things away. I never take tea.

Footman. Very good, m'm. (He hesitates.) I understood, m'm, that Mr. Oberville was to have tea?

Isabel. Mr. Oberville? But he was to arrive long ago! What time is it?

Footman. Only a quarter past five, m'm.

Isabel. A quarter past five? (She goes up to the clock.) Surely you're mistaken? I thought it was long after six. (To herself.) I walked and walked—I must have walked too fast ... (To the Footman.) I'm going out again. When Mr. Oberville arrives please give him his tea without waiting for me. I shall not be back till dinner-time.

Footman. Very good, m'm. Here are some letters, m'm.

Isabel (glancing at them with a movement of disgust). You may send them up to my room.

Footman. I beg pardon, m'm, but one is a note from Mme. Fanfreluche, and the man who brought it is waiting for an answer.

Isabel. Didn't you tell him I was out?

Footman. Yes, m'm. But he said he had orders to wait till you came in.

Isabel. Ah, let me see. (She opens the note.) Ah, yes. (A pause.) Please say that I am on my way now to Mme Fanfreluche's to give her the answer in person. You may tell the man that I have already started. Do you understand? Already started.

Footman. Yes, m'm.

Isabel. And—wait. (With an effort.) You may tell me when the man has started. I shall wait here till then. Be sure you let me know.

Footman. Yes, m'm. (He goes out.)

Isabel (sinking into a chair and hiding her face). Ah! (After a moment she rises, taking up her gloves and sunshade, and walks toward the window which opens on the lawn.) I'm so tired. (She hesitates and turns back into the room.) Where can I go to? (She sits down again by the tea- table, and bends over the kettle. The clock strikes half-past five.)

Isabel (picking up her sunshade, walks back to the window). If I must meet one of them...

Oberville (speaking in the hall). Thanks. I'll take tea first. (He enters the room, and pauses doubtfully on seeing Isabel.)

Isabel (stepping towards him with a smile). It's not that I've changed, of course, but only that I happened to have my back to the light. Isn't that what you are going to say?

Oberville. Mrs. Warland!

Isabel. So you really have become a great man! They always remember people's names.

Oberville. Were you afraid I was going to call you Isabel?

Isabel. Bravo! Crescendo!

Oberville. But you have changed, all the same.

Isabel. You must indeed have reached a dizzy eminence, since you can indulge yourself by speaking the truth!

Oberville. It's your voice. I knew it at once, and yet it's different.

Isabel. I hope it can still convey the pleasure I feel in seeing an old friend. (She holds out her hand. He takes it.) You know, I suppose, that Mrs. Raynor is not here to receive you? She was called away this morning very suddenly by her aunt's illness.

Oberville. Yes. She left a note for me. (Absently.) I'm sorry to hear of Mrs. Griscom's illness.

Isabel. Oh, Mrs. Griscom's illnesses are less alarming than her recoveries. But I am forgetting to offer you any tea. (She hands him a cup.) I remember you liked it very strong.

Oberville. What else do you remember?

Isabel. A number of equally useless things. My mind is a store-room of obsolete information.

Oberville. Why obsolete, since I am providing you with a use for it?

Isabel. At any rate, it's open to question whether it was worth storing for that length of time. Especially as there must have been others more fitted, by opportunity, to undertake the duty.

Oberville. The duty?

Isabel. Of remembering how you like your tea.

Oberville (with a change of tone). Since you call it a duty—I may remind you that it's one I have never asked anyone else to perform.

Isabel. As a duty! But as a pleasure?

Oberville. Do you really want to know?

Isabel. Oh, I don't require and charge you.

Oberville. You dislike as much as ever having the i's dotted?

Isabel. With a handwriting I know as well as yours!

Oberville (recovering his lightness of manner). Accomplished woman! (He examines her approvingly.) I'd no idea that you were here. I never was more surprised.

Isabel. I hope you like being surprised. To my mind it's an overrated pleasure.

Oberville. Is it? I'm sorry to hear that.

Isabel. Why? Have you a surprise to dispose of?

Oberville. I'm not sure that I haven't.

Isabel. Don't part with it too hastily. It may improve by being kept.

Oberville (tentatively). Does that mean that you don't want it?

Isabel. Heaven forbid! I want everything I can get.

Oberville. And you get everything you want. At least you used to.

Isabel. Let us talk of your surprise.

Oberville. It's to be yours, you know. (A pause. He speaks gravely.) I find that I've never got over having lost you.

Isabel (also gravely). And is that a surprise—to you too?

Oberville. Honestly, yes. I thought I'd crammed my life full. I didn't know there was a cranny left anywhere. At first, you know, I stuffed in everything I could lay my hands on, there was such a big void to fill. And after all I haven't filled it. I felt that the moment I saw you. (A pause.) I'm talking stupidly.

Isabel. It would be odious if you were eloquent.

Oberville. What do you mean?

Isabel. That's a question you never used to ask me.

Oberville. Be merciful. Remember how little practise I've had lately.

Isabel. In what?

Oberville. Never mind! (He rises and walks away; then comes back and stands in front of her.) What a fool I was to give you up!

Isabel. Oh, don't say that! I've lived on it!

Oberville. On my letting you go?

Isabel. On your letting everything go, but the right.

Oberville. Oh, hang the right! What is truth? We had the right to be happy!

Isabel (with rising emotion). I used to think so sometimes.

Oberville. Did you? Triple fool that I was!

Isabel. But you showed me—

Oberville. Why, good God, we belonged to each other—and I let you go! It's fabulous. I've fought for things since that weren't worth a crooked sixpence; fought as well as other men. And you—you—I lost you because I couldn't face a scene! Hang it, suppose there'd been a dozen scenes—I might have survived them. Men have been known to. They're not necessarily fatal.

Isabel. A scene?

Oberville. It's a form of fear that women don't understand. How you must have despised me!

Isabel. You were—afraid—of a scene?

Oberville. I was a damned coward, Isabel. That's about the size of it.

Isabel. Ah—I had thought it so much larger!

Oberville. What did you say?

Isabel. I said that you have forgotten to drink your tea. It must be quite cold.

Oberville. Ah—

Isabel. Let me give you another cup.

Oberville (collecting himself). No, no. This is perfect.

Isabel. You haven't tasted it.

Oberville (falling into her mood) . You always made it to perfection. Only you never gave me enough sugar.

Isabel. I know better now. (She puts another lump in his cup.)

Oberville (drinks his tea, and then says, with an air of reproach). Isn't all this chaff rather a waste of time between two old friends who haven't met for so many years?

Isabel (lightly). Oh, it's only a hors d'oeuvre, the tuning of the instruments. I'm out of practise too.

Oberville. Let us come to the grand air, then. (Sits down near her.) Tell me about yourself. What are you doing?

Isabel. At this moment? You'll never guess. I'm trying to remember you.

Oberville. To remember me?

Isabel. Until you came into the room just now my recollection of you was so vivid; you were a living whole in my thoughts. Now I am engaged in gathering up the fragments, in laboriously reconstructing you....

Oberville. I have changed so much, then?

Isabel. No, I don't believe that you've changed. It's only that I see you differently. Don't you know how hard it is to convince elderly people that the type of the evening paper is no smaller than when they were young?

Oberville. I've shrunk then?

Isabel. You couldn't have grown bigger. Oh, I'm serious now; you needn't prepare a smile. For years you were the tallest object on my horizon. I used to climb to the thought of you, as people who live in a flat country mount the church steeple for a view. It's wonderful how much I used to see from there! And the air was so strong and pure!

Oberville. And now?

Isabel. Now I can fancy how delightful it must be to sit next to you at dinner.

Oberville. You're unmerciful. Have I said anything to offend you?

Isabel. Of course not. How absurd!

Oberville. I lost my head a little, I forgot how long it is since we have met. When I saw you I forgot everything except what you had once been to me. (She is silent.) I thought you too generous to resent that. Perhaps I have overtaxed your generosity. (A pause.) Shall I confess it? When I first saw you I thought for a moment that you had remembered—as I had. You see I can only excuse myself by saying something inexcusable.

Isabel (deliberately). Not inexcusable.

Oberville. Not—?

Isabel. I had remembered.

Oberville. Isabel!

Isabel. But now—

Oberville. Ah, give me a moment before you unsay it!

Isabel. I don't mean to unsay it. There's no use in repealing an obsolete law. That's the pity of it! You say you lost me ten years ago. (A pause.) I never lost you till now.

Oberville. Now?

Isabel. Only this morning you were my supreme court of justice; there was no appeal from your verdict. Not an hour ago you decided a case for me—against myself! And now—. And the worst of it is that it's not because you've changed. How do I know if you've changed? You haven't said a hundred words to me. You haven't been an hour in the room. And the years must have enriched you, I daresay you've doubled your capital. You've been in the thick of life, and the metal you're made of brightens with use. Success on some men looks like a borrowed coat; it sits on you as though it had been made to order. I see all this; I know it; but I don't feel it. I don't feel anything... anywhere... I'm numb. (A pause.) Don't laugh, but I really don't think I should know now if you came into the room, unless I actually saw you. (They are both silent.)

Oberville (at length). Then, to put the most merciful interpretation upon your epigrams, your feeling for me was made out of poorer stuff than mine for you.

Isabel. Perhaps it has had harder wear.

Oberville. Or been less cared for?

Isabel. If one has only one cloak one must wear it in all weathers.

Oberville. Unless it is so beautiful and precious that one prefers to go cold and keep it under lock and key.

Isabel. In the cedar-chest of indifference, the key of which is usually lost.

Oberville. Ah, Isabel, you're too pat! How much I preferred your hesitations.

Isabel. My hesitations? That reminds me how much your coming has simplified things. I feel as if I'd had an auction sale of fallacies.

Oberville. You speak in enigmas, and I have a notion that your riddles are the reverse of the sphinx's, more dangerous to guess than to give up. And yet I used to find your thoughts such good reading.

Isabel. One cares so little for the style in which one's praises are written.

Oberville. You've been praising me for the last ten minutes and I find your style detestable. I would rather have you find fault with me like a friend than approve me like a dilettante.

Isabel. A dilettante! The very word I wanted!

Oberville. I am proud to have enriched so full a vocabulary. But I am still waiting for the word I want. (He grows serious.) Isabel, look in your heart—give me the first word you find there. You've no idea how much a beggar can buy with a penny!

Isabel. It's empty, my poor friend, it's empty.

Oberville. Beggars never say that to each other.

Isabel. No; never, unless it's true.

Oberville (after another silence). Why do you look at me so curiously?

Isabel. I'm—what was it you said? Approving you as a dilettante. Don't be alarmed; you can bear examination; I don't see a crack anywhere. After all, it's a satisfaction to find that one's idol makes a handsome bibelot.

Oberville (with an attempt at lightness). I was right then—you're a collector?

Isabel (modestly). One must make a beginning. I think I shall begin with you. (She smiles at him.) Positively, I must have you on my mantel- shelf! (She rises and looks at the clock.) But it's time to dress for dinner. (She holds out her hand to him and he kisses it. They look at each other, and it is clear that he does not quite understand, but is watching eagerly for his cue.)

Warland (coming in). Hullo, Isabel, you're here after all?

Isabel. And so is Mr. Oberville. (She looks straight at Warland.) I stayed in on purpose to meet him. My husband—(The two men bow.)

Warland (effusively). So glad to meet you. My wife talks of you so often. She's been looking forward tremendously to your visit.

Oberville. It's a long time since I've had the pleasure of seeing Mrs. Warland.

Isabel. But now we are going to make up for lost time. (As he goes to the door.) I claim you to-morrow for the whole day.

Oberville bows and goes out.

Isabel. Lucius... I think you'd better go to Washington, after all. (Musing.) Narragansett might do for the others, though.... Couldn't you get Fred Langham to ask all the rest of the party to go over there with him to-morrow morning? I shall have a headache and stay at home. (He looks at her doubtfully.) Mr. Oberville is a bad sailor.

Warland advances demonstratively.

Isabel (drawing back). It's time to go and dress. I think you said the black gown with spangles?

A CUP OF COLD WATER

I

It was three o'clock in the morning, and the cotillion was at its height, when Woburn left the over-heated splendor of the Gildermere ballroom, and after a delay caused by the determination of the drowsy footman to give him a ready-made overcoat with an imitation astrachan collar in place of his own unimpeachable Poole garment, found himself breasting the icy solitude of the Fifth Avenue. He was still smiling, as he emerged from the awning, at his insistence in claiming his own overcoat: it illustrated, humorously enough, the invincible force of habit. As he faced the wind, however, he discerned a providence in his persistency, for his coat was fur-lined, and he had a cold voyage before him on the morrow.

It had rained hard during the earlier part of the night, and the carriages waiting in triple line before the Gildermeres' door were still domed by shining umbrellas, while the electric lamps extending down the avenue blinked Narcissus-like at their watery images in the hollows of the sidewalk. A dry blast had come out of the north, with pledge of frost before daylight, and to Woburn's shivering fancy the pools in the pavement seemed already stiffening into ice. He turned up his coat-collar and stepped out rapidly, his hands deep in his coat-pockets.

As he walked he glanced curiously up at the ladder-like door-steps which may well suggest to the future archaeologist that all the streets of New York were once canals; at the spectral tracery of the trees about St. Luke's, the fretted mass of the Cathedral, and the mean vista of the long side-streets. The knowledge that he was perhaps looking at it all for the last time caused every detail to start out like a challenge to memory, and lit the brown-stone house-fronts with the glamor of sword-barred Edens.

It was an odd impulse that had led him that night to the Gildermere ball; but the same change in his condition which made him stare wonderingly at the houses in the Fifth Avenue gave the thrill of an exploit to the tame business of ball-going. Who would have imagined, Woburn mused, that such a situation as his would possess the priceless quality of sharpening the blunt edge of habit?

It was certainly curious to reflect, as he leaned against the doorway of Mrs. Gildermere's ball-room, enveloped in the warm atmosphere of the accustomed, that twenty-four hours later the people brushing by him with looks of friendly recognition would start at the thought of having seen him and slur over the recollection of having taken his hand!

And the girl he had gone there to see: what would she think of him? He knew well enough that her trenchant classifications of life admitted no overlapping of good and evil, made no allowance for that incalculable interplay of motives that justifies the subtlest casuistry of compassion. Miss Talcott was too young to distinguish the intermediate tints of the moral spectrum; and her judgments were further simplified by a peculiar concreteness of mind. Her bringing-up had fostered this tendency and she was surrounded by people who focussed life in the same way. To the girls in Miss Talcott's set, the attentions of a clever man who had to work for his living had the zest of a forbidden pleasure; but to marry such a man would be as unpardonable as to have one's carriage seen at the door of a cheap dress-maker. Poverty might make a man fascinating; but a settled income was the best evidence of stability of character. If there were anything in heredity, how could a nice girl trust a man whose parents had been careless enough to leave him unprovided for?

Neither Miss Talcott nor any of her friends could be charged with formulating these views; but they were implicit in the slope of every white shoulder and in the ripple of every yard of imported tulle dappling the foreground of Mrs. Gildermere's ball-room. The advantages of line and colour in veiling the crudities of a creed are obvious to emotional minds; and besides, Woburn was conscious that it was to the cheerful materialism of their parents that the young girls he admired owed that fine distinction of outline in which their skilfully-rippled hair and skilfully-hung draperies cooeperated with the slimness and erectness that came of participating in the most expensive sports, eating the most expensive food and breathing the most expensive air. Since the process which had produced them was so costly, how could they help being costly themselves? Woburn was too logical to expect to give no more for a piece of old Sevres than for a bit of kitchen crockery; he had no faith in wonderful bargains, and believed that one got in life just what one was willing to pay for. He had no mind to dispute the taste of those who preferred the rustic simplicity of the earthen crock; but his own fancy inclined to the piece of pate tendre which must be kept in a glass case and handled as delicately as a flower.

It was not merely by the external grace of these drawing-room ornaments that Woburn's sensibilities were charmed. His imagination was touched by the curious exoticism of view resulting from such conditions; He had always enjoyed listening to Miss Talcott even more than looking at her. Her ideas had the brilliant bloom and audacious irrelevance of those tropical orchids which strike root in air. Miss Talcott's opinions had no connection with the actual; her very materialism had the grace of artificiality. Woburn had been enchanted once by seeing her helpless before a smoking lamp: she had been obliged to ring for a servant because she did not know how to put it out.

Her supreme charm was the simplicity that comes of taking it for granted that people are born with carriages and country-places: it never occurred to her that such congenital attributes could be matter for self- consciousness, and she had none of the nouveau riche prudery which classes poverty with the nude in art and is not sure how to behave in the presence of either.

The conditions of Woburn's own life had made him peculiarly susceptible to those forms of elegance which are the flower of ease. His father had lost a comfortable property through sheer inability to go over his agent's accounts; and this disaster, coming at the outset of Woburn's school-days, had given a new bent to the family temperament. The father characteristically died when the effort of living might have made it possible to retrieve his fortunes; and Woburn's mother and sister, embittered by this final evasion, settled down to a vindictive war with circumstances. They were the kind of women who think that it lightens the burden of life to throw over the amenities, as a reduced housekeeper puts away her knick-knacks to make the dusting easier. They fought mean conditions meanly; but Woburn, in his resentment of their attitude, did not allow for the suffering which had brought it about: his own tendency was to overcome difficulties by conciliation rather than by conflict. Such surroundings threw into vivid relief the charming figure of Miss Talcott. Woburn instinctively associated poverty with bad food, ugly furniture, complaints and recriminations: it was natural that he should be drawn toward the luminous atmosphere where life was a series of peaceful and good-humored acts, unimpeded by petty obstacles. To spend one's time in such society gave one the illusion of unlimited credit; and also, unhappily, created the need for it.

It was here in fact that Woburn's difficulties began. To marry Miss Talcott it was necessary to be a rich man: even to dine out in her set involved certain minor extravagances. Woburn had determined to marry her sooner or later; and in the meanwhile to be with her as much as possible.

As he stood leaning in the doorway of the Gildermere ball-room, watching her pass him in the waltz, he tried to remember how it had begun. First there had been the tailor's bill; the fur-lined overcoat with cuffs and collar of Alaska sable had alone cost more than he had spent on his clothes for two or three years previously. Then there were theatre- tickets; cab-fares; florist's bills; tips to servants at the country- houses where he went because he knew that she was invited; the Omar Khayyam bound by Sullivan that he sent her at Christmas; the contributions to her pet charities; the reckless purchases at fairs where she had a stall. His whole way of life had imperceptibly changed and his year's salary was gone before the second quarter was due.

He had invested the few thousand dollars which had been his portion of his father's shrunken estate: when his debts began to pile up, he took a flyer in stocks and after a few months of varying luck his little patrimony disappeared. Meanwhile his courtship was proceeding at an inverse ratio to his financial ventures. Miss Talcott was growing tender and he began to feel that the game was in his hands. The nearness of the goal exasperated him. She was not the girl to wait and he knew that it must be now or never. A friend lent him five thousand dollars on his personal note and he bought railway stocks on margin. They went up and he held them for a higher rise: they fluctuated, dragged, dropped below the level at which he had bought, and slowly continued their uninterrupted descent. His broker called for more margin; he could not respond and was sold out.

What followed came about quite naturally. For several years he had been cashier in a well-known banking-house. When the note he had given his friend became due it was obviously necessary to pay it and he used the firm's money for the purpose. To repay the money thus taken, he increased his debt to his employers and bought more stocks; and on these operations he made a profit of ten thousand dollars. Miss Talcott rode in the Park, and he bought a smart hack for seven hundred, paid off his tradesmen, and went on speculating with the remainder of his profits. He made a little more, but failed to take advantage of the market and lost all that he had staked, including the amount taken from the firm. He increased his over- draft by another ten thousand and lost that; he over-drew a farther sum and lost again. Suddenly he woke to the fact that he owed his employers fifty thousand dollars and that the partners were to make their semi- annual inspection in two days. He realized then that within forty-eight hours what he had called borrowing would become theft.

There was no time to be lost: he must clear out and start life over again somewhere else. The day that he reached this decision he was to have met Miss Talcott at dinner. He went to the dinner, but she did not appear: she had a headache, his hostess explained. Well, he was not to have a last look at her, after all; better so, perhaps. He took leave early and on his way home stopped at a florist's and sent her a bunch of violets. The next morning he got a little note from her: the violets had done her head so much good, she would tell him all about it that evening at the Gildermere ball. Woburn laughed and tossed the note into the fire. That evening he would be on board ship: the examination of the books was to take place the following morning at ten. Woburn went down to the bank as usual; he did not want to do anything that might excite suspicion as to his plans, and from one or two questions which one of the partners had lately put to him he divined that he was being observed. At the bank the day passed uneventfully. He discharged his business with his accustomed care and went uptown at the usual hour.

In the first flush of his successful speculations he had set up bachelor lodgings, moved by the temptation to get away from the dismal atmosphere of home, from his mother's struggles with the cook and his sister's curiosity about his letters. He had been influenced also by the wish for surroundings more adapted to his tastes. He wanted to be able to give little teas, to which Miss Talcott might come with a married friend. She came once or twice and pronounced it all delightful: she thought it so nice to have only a few Whistler etchings on the walls and the simplest crushed levant for all one's books.

To these rooms Woburn returned on leaving the bank. His plans had taken definite shape. He had engaged passage on a steamer sailing for Halifax early the next morning; and there was nothing for him to do before going on board but to pack his clothes and tear up a few letters. He threw his clothes into a couple of portmanteaux, and when these had been called for by an expressman he emptied his pockets and counted up his ready money. He found that he possessed just fifty dollars and seventy-five cents; but his passage to Halifax was paid, and once there he could pawn his watch and rings. This calculation completed, he unlocked his writing-table drawer and took out a handful of letters. They were notes from Miss Talcott. He read them over and threw them into the fire. On his table stood her photograph. He slipped it out of its frame and tossed it on top of the blazing letters. Having performed this rite, he got into his dress-clothes and went to a small French restaurant to dine.

He had meant to go on board the steamer immediately after dinner; but a sudden vision of introspective hours in a silent cabin made him call for the evening paper and run his eye over the list of theatres. It would be as easy to go on board at midnight as now.

He selected a new vaudeville and listened to it with surprising freshness of interest; but toward eleven o'clock he again began to dread the approaching necessity of going down to the steamer. There was something peculiarly unnerving in the idea of spending the rest of the night in a stifling cabin jammed against the side of a wharf.

He left the theatre and strolled across to the Fifth Avenue. It was now nearly midnight and a stream of carriages poured up town from the opera and the theatres. As he stood on the corner watching the familiar spectacle it occurred to him that many of the people driving by him in smart broughams and C-spring landaus were on their way to the Gildermere ball. He remembered Miss Talcott's note of the morning and wondered if she were in one of the passing carriages; she had spoken so confidently of meeting him at the ball. What if he should go and take a last look at her? There was really nothing to prevent it. He was not likely to run across any member of the firm: in Miss Talcott's set his social standing was good for another ten hours at least. He smiled in anticipation of her surprise at seeing him, and then reflected with a start that she would not be surprised at all.

His meditations were cut short by a fall of sleety rain, and hailing a hansom he gave the driver Mrs. Gildermere's address.

As he drove up the avenue he looked about him like a traveller in a strange city. The buildings which had been so unobtrusively familiar stood out with sudden distinctness: he noticed a hundred details which had escaped his observation. The people on the sidewalks looked like strangers: he wondered where they were going and tried to picture the lives they led; but his own relation to life had been so suddenly reversed that he found it impossible to recover his mental perspective.

At one corner he saw a shabby man lurking in the shadow of the side street; as the hansom passed, a policeman ordered him to move on. Farther on, Woburn noticed a woman crouching on the door-step of a handsome house. She had drawn a shawl over her head and was sunk in the apathy of despair or drink. A well-dressed couple paused to look at her. The electric globe at the corner lit up their faces, and Woburn saw the lady, who was young and pretty, turn away with a little grimace, drawing her companion after her.

The desire to see Miss Talcott had driven Woburn to the Gildermeres'; but once in the ball-room he made no effort to find her. The people about him seemed more like strangers than those he had passed in the street. He stood in the doorway, studying the petty manoeuvres of the women and the resigned amenities of their partners. Was it possible that these were his friends? These mincing women, all paint and dye and whalebone, these apathetic men who looked as much alike as the figures that children cut out of a folded sheet of paper? Was it to live among such puppets that he had sold his soul? What had any of these people done that was noble, exceptional, distinguished? Who knew them by name even, except their tradesmen and the society reporters? Who were they, that they should sit in judgment on him?

The bald man with the globular stomach, who stood at Mrs. Gildermere's elbow surveying the dancers, was old Boylston, who had made his pile in wrecking railroads; the smooth chap with glazed eyes, at whom a pretty girl smiled up so confidingly, was Collerton, the political lawyer, who had been mixed up to his own advantage in an ugly lobbying transaction; near him stood Brice Lyndham, whose recent failure had ruined his friends and associates, but had not visibly affected the welfare of his large and expensive family. The slim fellow dancing with Miss Gildermere was Alec Vance, who lived on a salary of five thousand a year, but whose wife was such a good manager that they kept a brougham and victoria and always put in their season at Newport and their spring trip to Europe. The little ferret-faced youth in the corner was Regie Colby, who wrote the Entre- Nous paragraphs in the Social Searchlight: the women were charming to him and he got all the financial tips he wanted from their husbands and fathers.

And the women? Well, the women knew all about the men, and flattered them and married them and tried to catch them for their daughters. It was a domino-party at which the guests were forbidden to unmask, though they all saw through each other's disguises.

And these were the people who, within twenty-four hours, would be agreeing that they had always felt there was something wrong about Woburn! They would be extremely sorry for him, of course, poor devil; but there are certain standards, after all, what would society be without standards? His new friends, his future associates, were the suspicious-looking man whom the policeman had ordered to move on, and the drunken woman asleep on the door-step. To these he was linked by the freemasonry of failure.

Miss Talcott passed him on Collerton's arm; she was giving him one of the smiles of which Woburn had fancied himself sole owner. Collerton was a sharp fellow; he must have made a lot in that last deal; probably she would marry him. How much did she know about the transaction? She was a shrewd girl and her father was in Wall Street. If Woburn's luck had turned the other way she might have married him instead; and if he had confessed his sin to her one evening, as they drove home from the opera in their new brougham, she would have said that really it was of no use to tell her, for she never could understand about business, but that she did entreat him in future to be nicer to Regie Colby. Even now, if he made a big strike somewhere, and came back in ten years with a beard and a steam yacht, they would all deny that anything had been proved against him, and Mrs. Collerton might blush and remind him of their friendship. Well, why not? Was not all morality based on a convention? What was the stanchest code of ethics but a trunk with a series of false bottoms? Now and then one had the illusion of getting down to absolute right or wrong, but it was only a false bottom, a removable hypothesis, with another false bottom underneath. There was no getting beyond the relative.

The cotillion had begun. Miss Talcott sat nearly opposite him: she was dancing with young Boylston and giving him a Woburn-Collerton smile. So young Boylston was in the syndicate too!

Presently Woburn was aware that she had forgotten young Boylston and was glancing absently about the room. She was looking for someone, and meant the someone to know it: he knew that Lost-Chord look in her eyes.

A new figure was being formed. The partners circled about the room and Miss Talcott's flying tulle drifted close to him as she passed. Then the favors were distributed; white skirts wavered across the floor like thistle-down on summer air; men rose from their seats and fresh couples filled the shining parquet.

Miss Talcott, after taking from the basket a Legion of Honor in red enamel, surveyed the room for a moment; then she made her way through the dancers and held out the favor to Woburn. He fastened it in his coat, and emerging from the crowd of men about the doorway, slipped his arm about her. Their eyes met; hers were serious and a little sad. How fine and slender she was! He noticed the little tendrils of hair about the pink convolution of her ear. Her waist was firm and yet elastic; she breathed calmly and regularly, as though dancing were her natural motion. She did not look at him again and neither of them spoke.

When the music ceased they paused near her chair. Her partner was waiting for her and Woburn left her with a bow.

He made his way down-stairs and out of the house. He was glad that he had not spoken to Miss Talcott. There had been a healing power in their silence. All bitterness had gone from him and he thought of her now quite simply, as the girl he loved.

At Thirty-fifth Street he reflected that he had better jump into a car and go down to his steamer. Again there rose before him the repulsive vision of the dark cabin, with creaking noises overhead, and the cold wash of water against the pier: he thought he would stop in a cafe and take a drink. He turned into Broadway and entered a brightly-lit cafe; but when he had taken his whisky and soda there seemed no reason for lingering. He had never been the kind of man who could escape difficulties in that way. Yet he was conscious that his will was weakening; that he did not mean to go down to the steamer just yet. What did he mean to do? He began to feel horribly tired and it occurred to him that a few hours' sleep in a decent bed would make a new man of him. Why not go on board the next morning at daylight?

He could not go back to his rooms, for on leaving the house he had taken the precaution of dropping his latch-key into his letter-box; but he was in a neighborhood of discreet hotels and he wandered on till he came to one which was known to offer a dispassionate hospitality to luggageless travellers in dress-clothes.

II

He pushed open the swinging door and found himself in a long corridor with a tessellated floor, at the end of which, in a brightly-lit enclosure of plate-glass and mahogany, the night-clerk dozed over a copy of the Police Gazette. The air in the corridor was rich in reminiscences of yesterday's dinners, and a bronzed radiator poured a wave of dry heat into Woburn's face.

The night-clerk, roused by the swinging of the door, sat watching Woburn's approach with the unexpectant eye of one who has full confidence in his capacity for digesting surprises. Not that there was anything surprising in Woburn's appearance; but the night-clerk's callers were given to such imaginative flights in explaining their luggageless arrival in the small hours of the morning, that he fared habitually on fictions which would have staggered a less experienced stomach. The night-clerk, whose unwrinkled bloom showed that he throve on this high-seasoned diet, had a fancy for classifying his applicants before they could frame their explanations.

"This one's been locked out," he said to himself as he mustered Woburn.

Having exercised his powers of divination with his accustomed accuracy he listened without stirring an eye-lid to Woburn's statement; merely replying, when the latter asked the price of a room, "Two-fifty."

"Very well," said Woburn, pushing the money under the brass lattice, "I'll go up at once; and I want to be called at seven."

To this the night-clerk proffered no reply, but stretching out his hand to press an electric button, returned apathetically to the perusal of the Police Gazette. His summons was answered by the appearance of a man in shirt-sleeves, whose rumpled head indicated that he had recently risen from some kind of makeshift repose; to him the night-clerk tossed a key, with the brief comment, "Ninety-seven;" and the man, after a sleepy glance at Woburn, turned on his heel and lounged toward the staircase at the back of the corridor.

Woburn followed and they climbed three flights in silence. At each landing Woburn glanced down, the long passage-way lit by a lowered gas-jet, with a double line of boots before the doors, waiting, like yesterday's deeds, to carry their owners so many miles farther on the morrow's destined road. On the third landing the man paused, and after examining the number on the key, turned to the left, and slouching past three or four doors, finally unlocked one and preceded Woburn into a room lit only by the upward gleam of the electric globes in the street below.

The man felt in his pockets; then he turned to Woburn. "Got a match?" he asked.

Woburn politely offered him one, and he applied it to the gas-fixture which extended its jointed arm above an ash dressing-table with a blurred mirror fixed between two standards. Having performed this office with an air of detachment designed to make Woburn recognize it as an act of supererogation, he turned without a word and vanished down the passage- way.

Woburn, after an indifferent glance about the room, which seemed to afford the amount of luxury generally obtainable for two dollars and a half in a fashionable quarter of New York, locked the door and sat down at the ink- stained writing-table in the window. Far below him lay the pallidly-lit depths of the forsaken thoroughfare. Now and then he heard the jingle of a horsecar and the ring of hoofs on the freezing pavement, or saw the lonely figure of a policeman eclipsing the illumination of the plate-glass windows on the opposite side of the street. He sat thus for a long time, his elbows on the table, his chin between his hands, till at length the contemplation of the abandoned sidewalks, above which the electric globes kept Stylites-like vigil, became intolerable to him, and he drew down the window-shade, and lit the gas-fixture beside the dressing-table. Then he took a cigar from his case, and held it to the flame.

The passage from the stinging freshness of the night to the stale overheated atmosphere of the Haslemere Hotel had checked the preternaturally rapid working of his mind, and he was now scarcely conscious of thinking at all. His head was heavy, and he would have thrown himself on the bed had he not feared to oversleep the hour fixed for his departure. He thought it safest, instead, to seat himself once more by the table, in the most uncomfortable chair that he could find, and smoke one cigar after another till the first sign of dawn should give an excuse for action.

He had laid his watch on the table before him, and was gazing at the hour- hand, and trying to convince himself by so doing that he was still wide awake, when a noise in the adjoining room suddenly straightened him in his chair and banished all fear of sleep.

There was no mistaking the nature of the noise; it was that of a woman's sobs. The sobs were not loud, but the sound reached him distinctly through the frail door between the two rooms; it expressed an utter abandonment to grief; not the cloud-burst of some passing emotion, but the slow down-pour of a whole heaven of sorrow.

Woburn sat listening. There was nothing else to be done; and at least his listening was a mute tribute to the trouble he was powerless to relieve. It roused, too, the drugged pulses of his own grief: he was touched by the chance propinquity of two alien sorrows in a great city throbbing with multifarious passions. It would have been more in keeping with the irony of life had he found himself next to a mother singing her child to sleep: there seemed a mute commiseration in the hand that had led him to such neighborhood.

Gradually the sobs subsided, with pauses betokening an effort at self- control. At last they died off softly, like the intermittent drops that end a day of rain.

"Poor soul," Woburn mused, "she's got the better of it for the time. I wonder what it's all about?"

At the same moment he heard another sound that made him jump to his feet. It was a very low sound, but in that nocturnal silence which gives distinctness to the faintest noises, Woburn knew at once that he had heard the click of a pistol.

"What is she up to now?" he asked himself, with his eye on the door between the two rooms; and the brightly-lit keyhole seemed to reply with a glance of intelligence. He turned out the gas and crept to the door, pressing his eye to the illuminated circle.

After a moment or two of adjustment, during which he seemed to himself to be breathing like a steam-engine, he discerned a room like his own, with the same dressing-table flanked by gas-fixtures, and the same table in the window. This table was directly in his line of vision; and beside it stood a woman with a small revolver in her hands. The lights being behind her, Woburn could only infer her youth from her slender silhouette and the nimbus of fair hair defining her head. Her dress seemed dark and simple, and on a chair under one of the gas-jets lay a jacket edged with cheap fur and a small travelling-bag. He could not see the other end of the room, but something in her manner told him that she was alone. At length she put the revolver down and took up a letter that lay on the table. She drew the letter from its envelope and read it over two or three times; then she put it back, sealing the envelope, and placing it conspicuously against the mirror of the dressing-table.

There was so grave a significance in this dumb-show that Woburn felt sure that her next act would be to return to the table and take up the revolver; but he had not reckoned on the vanity of woman. After putting the letter in place she still lingered at the mirror, standing a little sideways, so that he could now see her face, which was distinctly pretty, but of a small and unelastic mould, inadequate to the expression of the larger emotions. For some moments she continued to study herself with the expression of a child looking at a playmate who has been scolded; then she turned to the table and lifted the revolver to her forehead.

A sudden crash made her arm drop, and sent her darting backward to the opposite side of the room. Woburn had broken down the door, and stood torn and breathless in the breach.

"Oh!" she gasped, pressing closer to the wall.

"Don't be frightened," he said; "I saw what you were going to do and I had to stop you."

She looked at him for a moment in silence, and he saw the terrified flutter of her breast; then she said, "No one can stop me for long. And besides, what right have you—"

"Everyone has the right to prevent a crime," he returned, the sound of the last word sending the blood to his forehead.

"I deny it," she said passionately. "Everyone who has tried to live and failed has the right to die."

"Failed in what?"

"In everything!" she replied. They stood looking at each other in silence.

At length he advanced a few steps.

"You've no right to say you've failed," he said, "while you have breath to try again." He drew the revolver from her hand.

"Try again—try again? I tell you I've tried seventy times seven!"

"What have you tried?"

She looked at him with a certain dignity.

"I don't know," she said, "that you've any right to question me—or to be in this room at all—" and suddenly she burst into tears.

The discrepancy between her words and action struck the chord which, in a man's heart, always responds to the touch of feminine unreason. She dropped into the nearest chair, hiding her face in her hands, while Woburn watched the course of her weeping.

At last she lifted her head, looking up between drenched lashes.

"Please go away," she said in childish entreaty.

"How can I?" he returned. "It's impossible that I should leave you in this state. Trust me, let me help you. Tell me what has gone wrong, and let's see if there's no other way out of it."

Woburn had a voice full of sensitive inflections, and it was now trembling with profoundest pity. Its note seemed to reassure the girl, for she said, with a beginning of confidence in her own tones, "But I don't even know who you are."

Woburn was silent: the words startled him. He moved nearer to her and went on in the same quieting tone.

"I am a man who has suffered enough to want to help others. I don't want to know any more about you than will enable me to do what I can for you. I've probably seen more of life than you have, and if you're willing to tell me your troubles perhaps together we may find a way out of them."

She dried her eyes and glanced at the revolver.

"That's the only way out," she said.

"How do you know? Are you sure you've tried every other?"

"Perfectly sure, I've written and written, and humbled myself like a slave before him, and she won't even let him answer my letters. Oh, but you don't understand"—she broke off with a renewal of weeping.

"I begin to understand, you're sorry for something you've done?"

"Oh, I've never denied that, I've never denied that I was wicked."

"And you want the forgiveness of someone you care about?"

"My husband," she whispered.

"You've done something to displease your husband?"

"To displease him? I ran away with another man!" There was a dismal exultation in her tone, as though she were paying Woburn off for having underrated her offense.

She had certainly surprised him; at worst he had expected a quarrel over a rival, with a possible complication of mother-in-law. He wondered how such helpless little feet could have taken so bold a step; then he remembered that there is no audacity like that of weakness.

He was wondering how to lead her to completer avowal when she added forlornly, "You see there's nothing else to do."

Woburn took a turn in the room. It was certainly a narrower strait than he had foreseen, and he hardly knew how to answer; but the first flow of confession had eased her, and she went on without farther persuasion.

"I don't know how I could ever have done it; I must have been downright crazy. I didn't care much for Joe when I married him, he wasn't exactly handsome, and girls think such a lot of that. But he just laid down and worshipped me, and I was getting fond of him in a way; only the life was so dull. I'd been used to a big city, I come from Detroit, and Hinksville is such a poky little place; that's where we lived; Joe is telegraph- operator on the railroad there. He'd have been in a much bigger place now, if he hadn't, well, after all, he behaved perfectly splendidly about that.

"I really was getting fond of him, and I believe I should have realized in time how good and noble and unselfish he was, if his mother hadn't been always sitting there and everlastingly telling me so. We learned in school about the Athenians hating some man who was always called just, and that's the way I felt about Joe. Whenever I did anything that wasn't quite right his mother would say how differently Joe would have done it. And she was forever telling me that Joe didn't approve of this and that and the other. When we were alone he approved of everything, but when his mother was round he'd sit quiet and let her say he didn't. I knew he'd let me have my way afterwards, but somehow that didn't prevent my getting mad at the time.

"And then the evenings were so long, with Joe away, and Mrs. Glenn (that's his mother) sitting there like an image knitting socks for the heathen. The only caller we ever had was the Baptist minister, and he never took any more notice of me than if I'd been a piece of furniture. I believe he was afraid to before Mrs. Glenn."

She paused breathlessly, and the tears in her eyes were now of anger.

"Well?" said Woburn gently.

"Well—then Arthur Hackett came along; he was travelling for a big publishing firm in Philadelphia. He was awfully handsome and as clever and sarcastic as anything. He used to lend me lots of novels and magazines, and tell me all about society life in New York. All the girls were after him, and Alice Sprague, whose father is the richest man in Hinksville, fell desperately in love with him and carried on like a fool; but he wouldn't take any notice of her. He never looked at anybody but me." Her face lit up with a reminiscent smile, and then clouded again. "I hate him now," she exclaimed, with a change of tone that startled Woburn. "I'd like to kill him, but he's killed me instead.

"Well, he bewitched me so I didn't know what I was doing; I was like somebody in a trance. When he wasn't there I didn't want to speak to anybody; I used to lie in bed half the day just to get away from folks; I hated Joe and Hinksville and everything else. When he came back the days went like a flash; we were together nearly all the time. I knew Joe's mother was spying on us, but I didn't care. And at last it seemed as if I couldn't let him go away again without me; so one evening he stopped at the back gate in a buggy, and we drove off together and caught the eastern express at River Bend. He promised to bring me to New York." She paused, and then added scornfully, "He didn't even do that!"

Woburn had returned to his seat and was watching her attentively. It was curious to note how her passion was spending itself in words; he saw that she would never kill herself while she had any one to talk to.

"That was five months ago," she continued, "and we travelled all through the southern states, and stayed a little while near Philadelphia, where his business is. He did things real stylishly at first. Then he was sent to Albany, and we stayed a week at the Delavan House. One afternoon I went out to do some shopping, and when I came back he was gone. He had taken his trunk with him, and hadn't left any address; but in my travelling-bag I found a fifty-dollar bill, with a slip of paper on which he had written, 'No use coming after me; I'm married.' We'd been together less than four months, and I never saw him again.

"At first I couldn't believe it. I stayed on, thinking it was a joke, or that he'd feel sorry for me and come back. But he never came and never wrote me a line. Then I began to hate him, and to see what a wicked fool I'd been to leave Joe. I was so lonesome, I thought I'd go crazy. And I kept thinking how good and patient Joe had been, and how badly I'd used him, and how lovely it would be to be back in the little parlor at Hinksville, even with Mrs. Glenn and the minister talking about free-will and predestination. So at last I wrote to Joe. I wrote him the humblest letters you ever read, one after another; but I never got any answer.

"Finally I found I'd spent all my money, so I sold my watch and my rings, Joe gave me a lovely turquoise ring when we were married, and came to New York. I felt ashamed to stay alone any longer in Albany; I was afraid that some of Arthur's friends, who had met me with him on the road, might come there and recognize me. After I got here I wrote to Susy Price, a great friend of mine who lives at Hinksville, and she answered at once, and told me just what I had expected, that Joe was ready to forgive me and crazy to have me back, but that his mother wouldn't let him stir a step or write me a line, and that she and the minister were at him all day long, telling him how bad I was and what a sin it would be to forgive me. I got Susy's letter two or three days ago, and after that I saw it was no use writing to Joe. He'll never dare go against his mother and she watches him like a cat. I suppose I deserve it, but he might have given me another chance! I know he would if he could only see me."

Her voice had dropped from anger to lamentation, and her tears again overflowed.

Woburn looked at her with the pity one feels for a child who is suddenly confronted with the result of some unpremeditated naughtiness.

"But why not go back to Hinksville," he suggested, "if your husband is ready to forgive you? You could go to your friend's house, and once your husband knows you are there you can easily persuade him to see you."

"Perhaps I could, Susy thinks I could. But I can't go back; I haven't got a cent left."

"But surely you can borrow money? Can't you ask your friend to forward you the amount of your fare?"

She shook her head.

"Susy ain't well off; she couldn't raise five dollars, and it costs twenty-five to get back to Hinksville. And besides, what would become of me while I waited for the money? They'll turn me out of here to-morrow; I haven't paid my last week's board, and I haven't got anything to give them; my bag's empty; I've pawned everything."

"And don't you know anyone here who would lend you the money?"

"No; not a soul. At least I do know one gentleman; he's a friend of Arthur's, a Mr. Devine; he was staying at Rochester when we were there. I met him in the street the other day, and I didn't mean to speak to him, but he came up to me, and said he knew all about Arthur and how meanly he had behaved, and he wanted to know if he couldn't help me, I suppose he saw I was in trouble. He tried to persuade me to go and stay with his aunt, who has a lovely house right round here in Twenty-fourth Street; he must be very rich, for he offered to lend me as much money as I wanted."

"You didn't take it?"

"No," she returned; "I daresay he meant to be kind, but I didn't care to be beholden to any friend of Arthur's. He came here again yesterday, but I wouldn't see him, so he left a note giving me his aunt's address and saying she'd have a room ready for me at any time."

There was a long silence; she had dried her tears and sat looking at Woburn with eyes full of helpless reliance.

"Well," he said at length, "you did right not to take that man's money; but this isn't the only alternative," he added, pointing to the revolver.

"I don't know any other," she answered wearily. "I'm not smart enough to get employment; I can't make dresses or do type-writing, or any of the useful things they teach girls now; and besides, even if I could get work I couldn't stand the loneliness. I can never hold my head up again, I can't bear the disgrace. If I can't go back to Joe I'd rather be dead."

"And if you go back to Joe it will be all right?" Woburn suggested with a smile.

"Oh," she cried, her whole face alight, "if I could only go back to Joe!"

They were both silent again; Woburn sat with his hands in his pockets gazing at the floor. At length his silence seemed to rouse her to the unwontedness of the situation, and she rose from her seat, saying in a more constrained tone, "I don't know why I've told you all this."

"Because you believed that I would help you," Woburn answered, rising also; "and you were right; I'm going to send you home."

She colored vividly. "You told me I was right not to take Mr. Devine's money," she faltered.

"Yes," he answered, "but did Mr. Devine want to send you home?"

"He wanted me to wait at his aunt's a little while first and then write to Joe again."

"I don't—I want you to start tomorrow morning; this morning, I mean. I'll take you to the station and buy your ticket, and your husband can send me back the money."

"Oh, I can't—I can't—you mustn't—" she stammered, reddening and paling. "Besides, they'll never let me leave here without paying."

"How much do you owe?"

"Fourteen dollars."

"Very well; I'll pay that for you; you can leave me your revolver as a pledge. But you must start by the first train; have you any idea at what time it leaves the Grand Central?"

"I think there's one at eight."

He glanced at his watch.

"In less than two hours, then; it's after six now."

She stood before him with fascinated eyes.

"You must have a very strong will," she said. "When you talk like that you make me feel as if I had to do everything you say."

"Well, you must," said Woburn lightly. "Man was made to be obeyed."

"Oh, you're not like other men," she returned; "I never heard a voice like yours; it's so strong and kind. You must be a very good man; you remind me of Joe; I'm sure you've got just such a nature; and Joe is the best man I've ever seen."

Woburn made no reply, and she rambled on, with little pauses and fresh bursts of confidence.

"Joe's a real hero, you know; he did the most splendid thing you ever heard of. I think I began to tell you about it, but I didn't finish. I'll tell you now. It happened just after we were married; I was mad with him at the time, I'm afraid, but now I see how splendid he was. He'd been telegraph operator at Hinksville for four years and was hoping that he'd get promoted to a bigger place; but he was afraid to ask for a raise. Well, I was very sick with a bad attack of pneumonia and one night the doctor said he wasn't sure whether he could pull me through. When they sent word to Joe at the telegraph office he couldn't stand being away from me another minute. There was a poor consumptive boy always hanging round the station; Joe had taught him how to operate, just to help him along; so he left him in the office and tore home for half an hour, knowing he could get back before the eastern express came along.

"He hadn't been gone five minutes when a freight-train ran off the rails about a mile up the track. It was a very still night, and the boy heard the smash and shouting, and knew something had happened. He couldn't tell what it was, but the minute he heard it he sent a message over the wires like a flash, and caught the eastern express just as it was pulling out of the station above Hinksville. If he'd hesitated a second, or made any mistake, the express would have come on, and the loss of life would have been fearful. The next day the Hinksville papers were full of Operator Glenn's presence of mind; they all said he'd be promoted. That was early in November and Joe didn't hear anything from the company till the first of January. Meanwhile the boy had gone home to his father's farm out in the country, and before Christmas he was dead. Well, on New Year's day Joe got a notice from the company saying that his pay was to be raised, and that he was to be promoted to a big junction near Detroit, in recognition of his presence of mind in stopping the eastern express. It was just what we'd both been pining for and I was nearly wild with joy; but I noticed Joe didn't say much. He just telegraphed for leave, and the next day he went right up to Detroit and told the directors there what had really happened. When he came back he told us they'd suspended him; I cried every night for a week, and even his mother said he was a fool. After that we just lived on at Hinksville, and six months later the company took him back; but I don't suppose they'll ever promote him now."

Her voice again trembled with facile emotion.

"Wasn't it beautiful of him? Ain't he a real hero?" she said. "And I'm sure you'd behave just like him; you'd be just as gentle about little things, and you'd never move an inch about big ones. You'd never do a mean action, but you'd be sorry for people who did; I can see it in your face; that's why I trusted you right off."

Woburn's eyes were fixed on the window; he hardly seemed to hear her. At length he walked across the room and pulled up the shade. The electric lights were dissolving in the gray alembic of the dawn. A milk-cart rattled down the street and, like a witch returning late from the Sabbath, a stray cat whisked into an area. So rose the appointed day.

Woburn turned back, drawing from his pocket the roll of bills which he had thrust there with so different a purpose. He counted them out, and handed her fifteen dollars.

"That will pay for your board, including your breakfast this morning," he said. "We'll breakfast together presently if you like; and meanwhile suppose we sit down and watch the sunrise. I haven't seen it for years."

He pushed two chairs toward the window, and they sat down side by side. The light came gradually, with the icy reluctance of winter; at last a red disk pushed itself above the opposite house-tops and a long cold gleam slanted across their window. They did not talk much; there was a silencing awe in the spectacle.

Presently Woburn rose and looked again at his watch.

"I must go and cover up my dress-coat", he said, "and you had better put on your hat and jacket. We shall have to be starting in half an hour."

As he turned away she laid her hand on his arm.

"You haven't even told me your name," she said.

"No," he answered; "but if you get safely back to Joe you can call me Providence."

"But how am I to send you the money?"

"Oh—well, I'll write you a line in a day or two and give you my address; I don't know myself what it will be; I'm a wanderer on the face of the earth."

"But you must have my name if you mean to write to me."

"Well, what is your name?"

"Ruby Glenn. And I think, I almost think you might send the letter right to Joe's, send it to the Hinksville station."

"Very well."

"You promise?"

"Of course I promise."

He went back into his room, thinking how appropriate it was that she should have an absurd name like Ruby. As he re-entered the room, where the gas sickened in the daylight, it seemed to him that he was returning to some forgotten land; he had passed, with the last few hours, into a wholly new phase of consciousness. He put on his fur coat, turning up the collar and crossing the lapels to hide his white tie. Then he put his cigar-case in his pocket, turned out the gas, and, picking up his hat and stick, walked back through the open doorway.

Ruby Glenn had obediently prepared herself for departure and was standing before the mirror, patting her curls into place. Her eyes were still red, but she had the happy look of a child that has outslept its grief. On the floor he noticed the tattered fragments of the letter which, a few hours earlier, he had seen her place before the mirror.

"Shall we go down now?" he asked.

"Very well," she assented; then, with a quick movement, she stepped close to him, and putting her hands on his shoulders lifted her face to his.

"I believe you're the best man I ever knew," she said, "the very best, except Joe."

She drew back blushing deeply, and unlocked the door which led into the passage-way. Woburn picked up her bag, which she had forgotten, and followed her out of the room. They passed a frowzy chambermaid, who stared at them with a yawn. Before the doors the row of boots still waited; there was a faint new aroma of coffee mingling with the smell of vanished dinners, and a fresh blast of heat had begun to tingle through the radiators.

In the unventilated coffee-room they found a waiter who had the melancholy air of being the last survivor of an exterminated race, and who reluctantly brought them some tea made with water which had not boiled, and a supply of stale rolls and staler butter. On this meagre diet they fared in silence, Woburn occasionally glancing at his watch; at length he rose, telling his companion to go and pay her bill while he called a hansom. After all, there was no use in economizing his remaining dollars.

In a few moments she joined him under the portico of the hotel. The hansom stood waiting and he sprang in after her, calling to the driver to take them to the Forty-second Street station.

When they reached the station he found a seat for her and went to buy her ticket. There were several people ahead of him at the window, and when he had bought the ticket he found that it was time to put her in the train. She rose in answer to his glance, and together they walked down the long platform in the murky chill of the roofed-in air. He followed her into the railway carriage, making sure that she had her bag, and that the ticket was safe inside it; then he held out his hand, in its pearl-coloured evening glove: he felt that the people in the other seats were staring at them.

"Good-bye," he said.

"Good-bye," she answered, flushing gratefully. "I'll never forget, never. And you will write, won't you? Promise!"

"Of course, of course," he said, hastening from the carriage.

He retraced his way along the platform, passed through the dismal waiting-room and stepped out into the early sunshine. On the sidewalk outside the station he hesitated awhile; then he strolled slowly down Forty-second Street and, skirting the melancholy flank of the Reservoir, walked across Bryant Park. Finally he sat down on one of the benches near the Sixth Avenue and lit a cigar. The signs of life were multiplying around him; he watched the cars roll by with their increasing freight of dingy toilers, the shop-girls hurrying to their work, the children trudging schoolward, their small vague noses red with cold, their satchels clasped in woollen-gloved hands. There is nothing very imposing in the first stirring of a great city's activities; it is a slow reluctant process, like the waking of a heavy sleeper; but to Woburn's mood the sight of that obscure renewal of humble duties was more moving than the spectacle of an army with banners.

He sat for a long time, smoking the last cigar in his case, and murmuring to himself a line from Hamlet, the saddest, he thought, in the play—

For every man hath business and desire.

Suddenly an unpremeditated movement made him feel the pressure of Ruby Glenn's revolver in his pocket; it was like a devil's touch on his arm, and he sprang up hastily. In his other pocket there were just four dollars and fifty cents; but that didn't matter now. He had no thought of flight.

For a few minutes he loitered vaguely about the park; then the cold drove him on again, and with the rapidity born of a sudden resolve he began to walk down the Fifth Avenue towards his lodgings. He brushed past a maid-servant who was washing the vestibule and ran up stairs to his room. A fire was burning in the grate and his books and photographs greeted him cheerfully from the walls; the tranquil air of the whole room seemed to take it for granted that he meant to have his bath and breakfast and go down town as usual.

He threw off his coat and pulled the revolver out of his pocket; for some moments he held it curiously in his hand, bending over to examine it as Ruby Glenn had done; then he laid it in the top drawer of a small cabinet, and locking the drawer threw the key into the fire.

After that he went quietly about the usual business of his toilet. In taking off his dress-coat he noticed the Legion of Honor which Miss Talcott had given him at the ball. He pulled it out of his buttonhole and tossed it into the fire-place. When he had finished dressing he saw with surprise that it was nearly ten o'clock. Ruby Glenn was already two hours nearer home.

Woburn stood looking about the room of which he had thought to take final leave the night before; among the ashes beneath the grate he caught sight of a little white heap which symbolized to his fancy the remains of his brief correspondence with Miss Talcott. He roused himself from this unseasonable musing and with a final glance at the familiar setting of his past, turned to face the future which the last hours had prepared for him.

He went down stairs and stepped out of doors, hastening down the street towards Broadway as though he were late for an appointment. Every now and then he encountered an acquaintance, whom he greeted with a nod and smile; he carried his head high, and shunned no man's recognition.

At length he reached the doors of a tall granite building honey-combed with windows. He mounted the steps of the portico, and passing through the double doors of plate-glass, crossed a vestibule floored with mosaic to another glass door on which was emblazoned the name of the firm.

This door he also opened, entering a large room with wainscotted subdivisions, behind which appeared the stooping shoulders of a row of clerks.

As Woburn crossed the threshold a gray-haired man emerged from an inner office at the opposite end of the room.

At sight of Woburn he stopped short.

"Mr. Woburn!" he exclaimed; then he stepped nearer and added in a low tone: "I was requested to tell you when you came that the members of the firm are waiting; will you step into the private office?"

THE PORTRAIT

I

It was at Mrs. Mellish's, one Sunday afternoon last spring. We were talking over George Lillo's portraits, a collection of them was being shown at Durand-Ruel's, and a pretty woman had emphatically declared:—

"Nothing on earth would induce me to sit to him!"

There was a chorus of interrogations.

"Oh, because—he makes people look so horrid; the way one looks on board ship, or early in the morning, or when one's hair is out of curl and one knows it. I'd so much rather be done by Mr. Cumberton!"

Little Cumberton, the fashionable purveyor of rose-water pastels, stroked his moustache to hide a conscious smile.

"Lillo is a genius—that we must all admit," he said indulgently, as though condoning a friend's weakness; "but he has an unfortunate temperament. He has been denied the gift, so precious to an artist, of perceiving the ideal. He sees only the defects of his sitters; one might almost fancy that he takes a morbid pleasure in exaggerating their weak points, in painting them on their worst days; but I honestly believe he can't help himself. His peculiar limitations prevent his seeing anything but the most prosaic side of human nature—

"'A primrose by the river's brim
A yellow primrose is to him,
And it is nothing more.'"

Cumberton looked round to surprise an order in the eye of the lady whose sentiments he had so deftly interpreted, but poetry always made her uncomfortable, and her nomadic attention had strayed to other topics. His glance was tripped up by Mrs. Mellish.

"Limitations? But, my dear man, it's because he hasn't any limitations, because he doesn't wear the portrait-painter's conventional blinders, that we're all so afraid of being painted by him. It's not because he sees only one aspect of his sitters, it's because he selects the real, the typical one, as instinctively as a detective collars a pick-pocket in a crowd. If there's nothing to paint, no real person, he paints nothing; look at the sumptuous emptiness of his portrait of Mrs. Guy Awdrey" ("Why," the pretty woman perplexedly interjected, "that's the only nice picture he ever did!") "If there's one positive trait in a negative whole he brings it out in spite of himself; if it isn't a nice trait, so much the worse for the sitter; it isn't Lillo's fault: he's no more to blame than a mirror. Your other painters do the surface, he does the depths; they paint the ripples on the pond, he drags the bottom. He makes flesh seem as fortuitous as clothes. When I look at his portraits of fine ladies in pearls and velvet I seem to see a little naked cowering wisp of a soul sitting beside the big splendid body, like a poor relation in the darkest corner of an opera-box. But look at his pictures of really great people, how great they are! There's plenty of ideal there. Take his Professor Clyde; how clearly the man's history is written in those broad steady strokes of the brush: the hard work, the endless patience, the fearless imagination of the great savant! Or the picture of Mr. Domfrey, the man who has felt beauty without having the power to create it. The very brush- work expresses the difference between the two; the crowding of nervous tentative lines, the subtler gradations of color, somehow convey a suggestion of dilettantism. You feel what a delicate instrument the man is, how every sense has been tuned to the finest responsiveness." Mrs. Mellish paused, blushing a little at the echo of her own eloquence. "My advice is, don't let George Lillo paint you if you don't want to be found out, or to find yourself out. That's why I've never let him do me; I'm waiting for the day of judgment," she ended with a laugh.

Everyone but the pretty woman, whose eyes betrayed a quivering impatience to discuss clothes, had listened attentively to Mrs. Mellish. Lillo's presence in New York, he had come over from Paris for the first time in twelve years, to arrange the exhibition of his pictures, gave to the analysis of his methods as personal a flavor as though one had been furtively dissecting his domestic relations. The analogy, indeed, is not unapt; for in Lillo's curiously detached existence it is difficult to figure any closer tie than that which unites him to his pictures. In this light, Mrs. Mellish's flushed harangue seemed not unfitted to the trivialities of the tea hour, and some one almost at once carried on the argument by saying:—"But according to your theory—that the significance of his work depends on the significance of the sitter, his portrait of Vard ought to be a master-piece; and it's his biggest failure."

Alonzo Vard's suicide, he killed himself, strangely enough, the day that Lillo's pictures were first shown—had made his portrait the chief feature of the exhibition. It had been painted ten or twelve years earlier, when the terrible "Boss" was at the height of his power; and if ever man presented a type to stimulate such insight as Lillo's, that man was Vard; yet the portrait was a failure. It was magnificently composed; the technique was dazzling; but the face had been, well, expurgated. It was Vard as Cumberton might have painted him, a common man trying to look at ease in a good coat. The picture had never before been exhibited, and there was a general outcry of disappointment. It wasn't only the critics and the artists who grumbled. Even the big public, which had gaped and shuddered at Vard, revelling in his genial villany, and enjoying in his death that succumbing to divine wrath which, as a spectacle, is next best to its successful defiance, even the public felt itself defrauded. What had the painter done with their hero? Where was the big sneering domineering face that figured so convincingly in political cartoons and patent-medicine advertisements, on cigar-boxes and electioneering posters? They had admired the man for looking his part so boldly; for showing the undisguised blackguard in every line of his coarse body and cruel face; the pseudo-gentleman of Lillo's picture was a poor thing compared to the real Vard. It had been vaguely expected that the great boss's portrait would have the zest of an incriminating document, the scandalous attraction of secret memoirs; and instead, it was as insipid as an obituary. It was as though the artist had been in league with his sitter, had pledged himself to oppose to the lust for post-mortem "revelations" an impassable blank wall of negation. The public was resentful, the critics were aggrieved. Even Mrs. Mellish had to lay down her arms.

"Yes, the portrait of Vard is a failure," she admitted, "and I've never known why. If he'd been an obscure elusive type of villain, one could understand Lillo's missing the mark for once; but with that face from the pit—!"

She turned at the announcement of a name which our discussion had drowned, and found herself shaking hands with Lillo.

The pretty woman started and put her hands to her curls; Cumberton dropped a condescending eyelid (he never classed himself by recognizing degrees in the profession), and Mrs. Mellish, cheerfully aware that she had been overheard, said, as she made room for Lillo—

"I wish you'd explain it."

Lillo smoothed his beard and waited for a cup of tea. Then, "Would there be any failures," he said, "if one could explain them?"

"Ah, in some cases I can imagine it's impossible to seize the type, or to say why one has missed it. Some people are like daguerreotypes; in certain lights one can't see them at all. But surely Vard was obvious enough. What I want to know is, what became of him? What did you do with him? How did you manage to shuffle him out of sight?"

"It was much easier than you think. I simply missed an opportunity—"

"That a sign-painter would have seen!"

"Very likely. In fighting shy of the obvious one may miss the significant—"

"—And when I got back from Paris," the pretty woman was heard to wail, "I found all the women here were wearing the very models I'd brought home with me!"

Mrs. Mellish, as became a vigilant hostess, got up and shuffled her guests; and the question of Vard's portrait was dropped.

I left the house with Lillo; and on the way down Fifth Avenue, after one of his long silences, he suddenly asked:

"Is that what is generally said of my picture of Vard? I don't mean in the newspapers, but by the fellows who know?"

I said it was.

He drew a deep breath. "Well," he said, "it's good to know that when one tries to fail one can make such a complete success of it."

"Tries to fail?"

"Well, no; that's not quite it, either; I didn't want to make a failure of Vard's picture, but I did so deliberately, with my eyes open, all the same. It was what one might call a lucid failure."

"But why—?"

"The why of it is rather complicated. I'll tell you some time—" He hesitated. "Come and dine with me at the club by and by, and I'll tell you afterwards. It's a nice morsel for a psychologist."

At dinner he said little; but I didn't mind that. I had known him for years, and had always found something soothing and companionable in his long abstentions from speech. His silence was never unsocial; it was bland as a natural hush; one felt one's self included in it, not left out. He stroked his beard and gazed absently at me; and when we had finished our coffee and liqueurs we strolled down to his studio.

At the studio, which was less draped, less posed, less consciously "artistic" than those of the smaller men, he handed me a cigar, and fell to smoking before the fire. When he began to talk it was of indifferent matters, and I had dismissed the hope of hearing more of Vard's portrait, when my eye lit on a photograph of the picture. I walked across the room to look at it, and Lillo presently followed with a light.

"It certainly is a complete disguise," he muttered over my shoulder; then he turned away and stooped to a big portfolio propped against the wall.

"Did you ever know Miss Vard?" he asked, with his head in the portfolio; and without waiting for my answer he handed me a crayon sketch of a girl's profile.

I had never seen a crayon of Lillo's, and I lost sight of the sitter's personality in the interest aroused by this new aspect of the master's complex genius. The few lines, faint, yet how decisive!—flowered out of the rough paper with the lightness of opening petals. It was a mere hint of a picture, but vivid as some word that wakens long reverberations in the memory.

I felt Lillo at my shoulder again.

"You knew her, I suppose?"

I had to stop and think. Why, of course I'd known her: a silent handsome girl, showy yet ineffective, whom I had seen without seeing the winter that society had capitulated to Vard. Still looking at the crayon, I tried to trace some connection between the Miss Vard I recalled and the grave young seraph of Lillo's sketch. Had the Vards bewitched him? By what masterstroke of suggestion had he been beguiled into drawing the terrible father as a barber's block, the commonplace daughter as this memorable creature?

"You don't remember much about her? No, I suppose not. She was a quiet girl and nobody noticed her much, even when—" he paused with a smile—"you were all asking Vard to dine."

I winced. Yes, it was true, we had all asked Vard to dine. It was some comfort to think that fate had made him expiate our weakness.

Lillo put the sketch on the mantel-shelf and drew his arm-chair to the fire.

"It's cold to-night. Take another cigar, old man; and some whiskey? There ought to be a bottle and some glasses in that cupboard behind you... help yourself..."

II

About Vard's portrait? (he began.) Well, I'll tell you. It's a queer story, and most people wouldn't see anything in it. My enemies might say it was a roundabout way of explaining a failure; but you know better than that. Mrs. Mellish was right. Between me and Vard there could be no question of failure. The man was made for me, I felt that the first time I clapped eyes on him. I could hardly keep from asking him to sit to me on the spot; but somehow one couldn't ask favors of the fellow. I sat still and prayed he'd come to me, though; for I was looking for something big for the next Salon. It was twelve years ago, the last time I was out ere, and I was ravenous for an opportunity. I had the feeling, do you writer-fellows have it too?—that there was something tremendous in me if it could only be got out; and I felt Vard was the Moses to strike the rock. There were vulgar reasons, too, that made me hunger for a victim. I'd been grinding on obscurely for a good many years, without gold or glory, and the first thing of mine that had made a noise was my picture of Pepita, exhibited the year before. There'd been a lot of talk about that, orders were beginning to come in, and I wanted to follow it up with a rousing big thing at the next Salon. Then the critics had been insinuating that I could do only Spanish things, I suppose I had overdone the castanet business; it's a nursery-disease we all go through, and I wanted to show that I had plenty more shot in my locker. Don't you get up every morning meaning to prove you're equal to Balzac or Thackeray? That's the way I felt then; only give me a chance, I wanted to shout out to them; and I saw at once that Vard was my chance.

I had come over from Paris in the autumn to paint Mrs. Clingsborough, and I met Vard and his daughter at one of the first dinners I went to. After that I could think of nothing but that man's head. What a type! I raked up all the details of his scandalous history; and there were enough to fill an encyclopaedia. The papers were full of him just then; he was mud from head to foot; it was about the time of the big viaduct steal, and irreproachable citizens were forming ineffectual leagues to put him down. And all the time one kept meeting him at dinners, that was the beauty of it! Once I remember seeing him next to the Bishop's wife; I've got a little sketch of that duet somewhere... Well, he was simply magnificent; what a splendid condottiere he would have made, in gold armor, with a griffin grinning on his casque! You remember those drawings of Leonardo's, where the knight's face and the outline of his helmet combine in one monstrous saurian profile? He always reminded me of that...

But how was I to get at him?—One day it occurred to me to try talking to Miss Vard. She was a monosyllabic person, who didn't seem to see an inch beyond the last remark one had made; but suddenly I found myself blurting out, "I wonder if you know how extraordinarily paintable your father is?" and you should have seen the change that came over her. Her eyes lit up and she looked, well, as I've tried to make her look there. (He glanced up at the sketch.) Yes, she said, wasn't her father splendid, and didn't I think him one of the handsomest men I'd ever seen?

That rather staggered me, I confess; I couldn't think her capable of joking on such a subject, yet it seemed impossible that she should be speaking seriously. But she was. I knew it by the way she looked at Vard, who was sitting opposite, his wolfish profile thrown back, the shaggy locks tossed off his narrow high white forehead. The girl worshipped him.

She went on to say how glad she was that I saw him as she did. So many artists admired only regular beauty, the stupid Greek type that was made to be done in marble; but she'd always fancied from what she'd seen of my work, she knew everything I'd done, it appeared, that I looked deeper, cared more for the way in which faces are modelled by temperament and circumstance; "and of course in that sense," she concluded, "my father's face is beautiful."

This was even more staggering; but one couldn't question her divine sincerity. I'm afraid my one thought was to take advantage of it; and I let her go on, perceiving that if I wanted to paint Vard all I had to do was to listen.

She poured out her heart. It was a glorious thing for a girl, she said, wasn't it, to be associated with such a life as that? She felt it so strongly, sometimes, that it oppressed her, made her shy and stupid. She was so afraid people would expect her to live up to him. But that was absurd, of course; brilliant men so seldom had clever children. Still—did I know?—she would have been happier, much happier, if he hadn't been in public life; if he and she could have hidden themselves away somewhere, with their books and music, and she could have had it all to herself: his cleverness, his learning, his immense unbounded goodness. For no one knew how good he was; no one but herself. Everybody recognized his cleverness, his brilliant abilities; even his enemies had to admit his extraordinary intellectual gifts, and hated him the worse, of course, for the admission; but no one, no one could guess what he was at home. She had heard of great men who were always giving gala performances in public, but whose wives and daughters saw only the empty theatre, with the footlights out and the scenery stacked in the wings; but with him it was just the other way: wonderful as he was in public, in society, she sometimes felt he wasn't doing himself justice, he was so much more wonderful at home. It was like carrying a guilty secret about with her: his friends, his admirers, would never forgive her if they found out that he kept all his best things for her!

I don't quite know what I felt in listening to her. I was chiefly taken up with leading her on to the point I had in view; but even through my personal preoccupation I remember being struck by the fact that, though she talked foolishly, she didn't talk like a fool. She was not stupid; she was not obtuse; one felt that her impassive surface was alive with delicate points of perception; and this fact, coupled with her crystalline frankness, flung me back on a startled revision of my impressions of her father. He came out of the test more monstrous than ever, as an ugly image reflected in clear water is made uglier by the purity of the medium. Even then I felt a pang at the use to which fate had put the mountain-pool of Miss Vard's spirit, and an uneasy sense that my own reflection there was not one to linger over. It was odd that I should have scrupled to deceive, on one small point, a girl already so hugely cheated; perhaps it was the completeness of her delusion that gave it the sanctity of a religious belief. At any rate, a distinct sense of discomfort tempered the satisfaction with which, a day or two later, I heard from her that her father had consented to give me a few sittings.

I'm afraid my scruples vanished when I got him before my easel. He was immense, and he was unexplored. From my point of view he'd never been done before, I was his Cortez. As he talked the wonder grew. His daughter came with him, and I began to think she was right in saying that he kept his best for her. It wasn't that she drew him out, or guided the conversation; but one had a sense of delicate vigilance, hardly more perceptible than one of those atmospheric influences that give the pulses a happier turn. She was a vivifying climate. I had meant to turn the talk to public affairs, but it slipped toward books and art, and I was faintly aware of its being kept there without undue pressure. Before long I saw the value of the diversion. It was easy enough to get at the political Vard: the other aspect was rarer and more instructive. His daughter had described him as a scholar. He wasn't that, of course, in any intrinsic sense: like most men of his type he had gulped his knowledge standing, as he had snatched his food from lunch-counters; the wonder of it lay in his extraordinary power of assimilation. It was the strangest instance of a mind to which erudition had given force and fluency without culture; his learning had not educated his perceptions: it was an implement serving to slash others rather than to polish himself. I have said that at first sight he was immense; but as I studied him he began to lessen under my scrutiny. His depth was a false perspective painted on a wall.

It was there that my difficulty lay: I had prepared too big a canvas for him. Intellectually his scope was considerable, but it was like the digital reach of a mediocre pianist, it didn't make him a great musician. And morally he wasn't bad enough; his corruption wasn't sufficiently imaginative to be interesting. It was not so much a means to an end as a kind of virtuosity practised for its own sake, like a highly-developed skill in cannoning billiard balls. After all, the point of view is what gives distinction to either vice or virtue: a morality with ground-glass windows is no duller than a narrow cynicism.

His daughter's presence, she always came with him, gave unintentional emphasis to these conclusions; for where she was richest he was naked. She had a deep-rooted delicacy that drew color and perfume from the very centre of her being: his sentiments, good or bad, were as detachable as his cuffs. Thus her nearness, planned, as I guessed, with the tender intention of displaying, elucidating him, of making him accessible in detail to my dazzled perceptions, this pious design in fact defeated itself. She made him appear at his best, but she cheapened that best by her proximity. For the man was vulgar to the core; vulgar in spite of his force and magnitude; thin, hollow, spectacular; a lath-and-plaster bogey—

Did she suspect it? I think not—then. He was wrapped in her impervious faith... The papers? Oh, their charges were set down to political rivalry; and the only people she saw were his hangers-on, or the fashionable set who had taken him up for their amusement. Besides, she would never have found out in that way: at a direct accusation her resentment would have flamed up and smothered her judgment. If the truth came to her, it would come through knowing intimately some one—different; through—how shall I put it?—an imperceptible shifting of her centre of gravity. My besetting fear was that I couldn't count on her obtuseness. She wasn't what is called clever; she left that to him; but she was exquisitely good; and now and then she had intuitive felicities that frightened me. Do I make you see her? We fellows can explain better with the brush; I don't know how to mix my words or lay them on. She wasn't clever; but her heart thought—that's all I can say...

If she'd been stupid it would have been easy enough: I could have painted him as he was. Could have? I did—brushed the face in one day from memory; it was the very man! I painted it out before she came: I couldn't bear to have her see it. I had the feeling that I held her faith in him in my hands, carrying it like a brittle object through a jostling mob; a hair's-breadth swerve and it was in splinters.

When she wasn't there I tried to reason myself out of these subtleties. My business was to paint Vard as he was, if his daughter didn't mind his looks, why should I? The opportunity was magnificent, I knew that by the way his face had leapt out of the canvas at my first touch. It would have been a big thing. Before every sitting I swore to myself I'd do it; then she came, and sat near him, and I—didn't.

I knew that before long she'd notice I was shirking the face. Vard himself took little interest in the portrait, but she watched me closely, and one day when the sitting was over she stayed behind and asked me when I meant to begin what she called "the likeness." I guessed from her tone that the embarrassment was all on my side, or that if she felt any it was at having to touch a vulnerable point in my pride. Thus far the only doubt that troubled her was a distrust of my ability. Well, I put her off with any rot you please: told her she must trust me, must let me wait for the inspiration; that some day the face would come; I should see it suddenly—feel it under my brush... The poor child believed me: you can make a woman believe almost anything she doesn't quite understand. She was abashed at her philistinism, and begged me not to tell her father—he would make such fun of her!

After that, well, the sittings went on. Not many, of course; Vard was too busy to give me much time. Still, I could have done him ten times over. Never had I found my formula with such ease, such assurance; there were no hesitations, no obstructions, the face was there, waiting for me; at times it almost shaped itself on the canvas. Unfortunately Miss Vard was there too ...

All this time the papers were busy with the viaduct scandal. The outcry was getting louder. You remember the circumstances? One of Vard's associates—Bardwell, wasn't it?—threatened disclosures. The rival machine got hold of him, the Independents took him to their bosom, and the press shrieked for an investigation. It was not the first storm Vard had weathered, and his face wore just the right shade of cool vigilance; he wasn't the man to fall into the mistake of appearing too easy. His demeanor would have been superb if it had been inspired by a sense of his own strength; but it struck me rather as based on contempt for his antagonists. Success is an inverted telescope through which one's enemies are apt to look too small and too remote. As for Miss Vard, her serenity was undiminished; but I half-detected a defiance in her unruffled sweetness, and during the last sittings I had the factitious vivacity of a hostess who hears her best china crashing.

One day it did crash: the head-lines of the morning papers shouted the catastrophe at me:—"The Monster forced to disgorge, Warrant out against Vard, Bardwell the Boss's Boomerang"—you know the kind of thing.

When I had read the papers I threw them down and went out. As it happened, Vard was to have given me a sitting that morning; but there would have been a certain irony in waiting for him. I wished I had finished the picture, I wished I'd never thought of painting it. I wanted to shake off the whole business, to put it out of my mind, if I could: I had the feeling, I don't know if I can describe it, that there was a kind of disloyalty to the poor girl in my even acknowledging to myself that I knew what all the papers were howling from the housetops....

I had walked for an hour when it suddenly occurred to me that Miss Vard might, after all, come to the studio at the appointed hour. Why should she? I could conceive of no reason; but the mere thought of what, if she did come, my absence would imply to her, sent me bolting back to Twelfth Street. It was a presentiment, if you like, for she was there.

As she rose to meet me a newspaper slipped from her hand: I'd been fool enough, when I went out, to leave the damned things lying all over the place.

I muttered some apology for being late, and she said reassuringly:

"But my father's not here yet."

"Your father—?" I could have kicked myself for the way I bungled it!

"He went out very early this morning, and left word that he would meet me here at the usual hour."

She faced me, with an eye full of bright courage, across the newspaper lying between us.

"He ought to be here in a moment now, he's always so punctual. But my watch is a little fast, I think."

She held it out to me almost gaily, and I was just pretending to compare it with mine, when there was a smart rap on the door and Vard stalked in. There was always a civic majesty in his gait, an air of having just stepped off his pedestal and of dissembling an oration in his umbrella; and that day he surpassed himself. Miss Vard had turned pale at the knock; but the mere sight of him replenished her veins, and if she now avoided my eye, it was in mere pity for my discomfiture.

I was in fact the only one of the three who didn't instantly "play up"; but such virtuosity was inspiring, and by the time Vard had thrown off his coat and dropped into a senatorial pose, I was ready to pitch into my work. I swore I'd do his face then and there; do it as she saw it; she sat close to him, and I had only to glance at her while I painted —

Vard himself was masterly: his talk rattled through my hesitations and embarrassments like a brisk northwester sweeping the dry leaves from its path. Even his daughter showed the sudden brilliance of a lamp from which the shade has been removed. We were all surprisingly vivid, it felt, somehow, as though we were being photographed by flash-light...

It was the best sitting we'd ever had, but unfortunately it didn't last more than ten minutes.

It was Vard's secretary who interrupted us, a slinking chap called Cornley, who burst in, as white as sweetbread, with the face of a depositor who hears his bank has stopped payment. Miss Vard started up as he entered, but caught herself together and dropped back into her chair. Vard, who had taken out a cigarette, held the tip tranquilly to his fusee.

"You're here, thank God!" Cornley cried. "There's no time to be lost, Mr. Vard. I've got a carriage waiting round the corner in Thirteenth Street—"

Vard looked at the tip of his cigarette.

"A carriage in Thirteenth Street? My good fellow, my own brougham is at the door."

"I know, I know, but they're there too, sir; or they will be, inside of a minute. For God's sake, Mr. Vard, don't trifle! There's a way out by Thirteenth Street, I tell you"—

"Bardwell's myrmidons, eh?" said Vard. "Help me on with my overcoat, Cornley, will you?"

Cornley's teeth chattered.

"Mr. Vard, your best friends ... Miss Vard, won't you speak to your father?" He turned to me haggardly; "We can get out by the back way?"

I nodded.

Vard stood towering—in some infernal way he seemed literally to rise to the situation, one hand in the bosom of his coat, in the attitude of patriotism in bronze. I glanced at his daughter: she hung on him with a drowning look. Suddenly she straightened herself; there was something of Vard in the way she faced her fears, a kind of primitive calm we drawing- room folk don't have. She stepped to him and laid her hand on his arm. The pause hadn't lasted ten seconds.

"Father—" she said.

Vard threw back his head and swept the studio with a sovereign eye.

"The back way, Mr. Vard, the back way," Cornley whimpered. "For God's sake, sir, don't lose a minute."

Vard transfixed his abject henchman.

"I have never yet taken the back way," he enunciated; and, with a gesture matching the words, he turned to me and bowed.

"I regret the disturbance"—and he walked to the door. His daughter was at his side, alert, transfigured.

"Stay here, my dear."

"Never!"

They measured each other an instant; then he drew her arm in his. She flung back one look at me, a paean of victory, and they passed out with Cornley at their heels.

I wish I'd finished the face then; I believe I could have caught something of the look she had tried to make me see in him. Unluckily I was too excited to work that day or the next, and within the week the whole business came out. If the indictment wasn't a put-up job, and on that I believe there were two opinions, all that followed was. You remember the farcical trial, the packed jury, the compliant judge, the triumphant acquittal?... It's a spectacle that always carries conviction to the voter: Vard was never more popular than after his "exoneration"...

I didn't see Miss Vard for weeks. It was she who came to me at length; came to the studio alone, one afternoon at dusk. She had—what shall I say?—a veiled manner; as though she had dropped a fine gauze between us. I waited for her to speak.

She glanced about the room, admiring a hawthorn vase I had picked up at auction. Then, after a pause, she said:

"You haven't finished the picture?"

"Not quite," I said.

She asked to see it, and I wheeled out the easel and threw the drapery back.

"Oh," she murmured, "you haven't gone on with the face?"

I shook my head.

She looked down on her clasped hands and up at the picture; not once at me.

"You, you're going to finish it?"

"Of course," I cried, throwing the revived purpose into my voice. By God, I would finish it!

The merest tinge of relief stole over her face, faint as the first thin chirp before daylight.

"Is it so very difficult?" she asked tentatively.

"Not insuperably, I hope."

She sat silent, her eyes on the picture. At length, with an effort, she brought out: "Shall you want more sittings?"

For a second I blundered between two conflicting conjectures; then the truth came to me with a leap, and I cried out, "No, no more sittings!"

She looked up at me then for the first time; looked too soon, poor child; for in the spreading light of reassurance that made her eyes like a rainy dawn, I saw, with terrible distinctness, the rout of her disbanded hopes. I knew that she knew ...

I finished the picture and sent it home within a week. I tried to make it—what you see. Too late, you say? Yes—for her; but not for me or for the public. If she could be made to feel, for a day longer, for an hour even, that her miserable secret was a secret—why, she'd made it seem worth while to me to chuck my own ambitions for that ...

Lillo rose, and taking down the sketch stood looking at it in silence.

After a while I ventured, "And Miss Vard—?"

He opened the portfolio and put the sketch back, tying the strings with deliberation. Then, turning to relight his cigar at the lamp, he said: "She died last year, thank God."

Edith Wharton – A Short Biography

The extraordinary American writer Edith Wharton was born Edith Newbold Jones on January 24th, 1862 to George Frederic Jones and Lucretia Stevens Rhinelander at their brownstone at 14 West Twenty-third Street in New York City. Her parents already had two older sons, Frederic Rhinelander, and Henry Edward.

Edith was baptized April 20, 1862, Easter Sunday, at Grace Church. To her friends and family she was apparently known as "Pussy Jones".

The 1860's were a time of Civil War in America but by the time Edith was three the war was over and a more normal life among Americans could resume.

From 1866 to 1872, the Jones family visited France, Italy, Germany, and Spain and Edith became fluent in French, German, and Italian. She was taught by a succession of tutors and governesses. Her thirst for learning was apparent at even this early age. So too was a streak of rebelliousness as she pushed back at society's standards of fashion and etiquette that were thought to be needed to help these young women marry well and to be displayed at balls and parties. She thought this superficial and oppressive.

Although he mother forbade her to read novels until she married (Edith it seems complied with that instruction) she read from her father's library and that of friends.

Edith first step to becoming a writer was inventing stories when she was around six. She would walk around the living room holding a book and reciting her story.

In 1872 at age ten, Edith was taken ill with typhoid fever while the family was at a spa in the Black Forest. The family returned to the United States that same year to begin a cycle of winters in New York and their summers in Newport, Rhode Island.

The following year, 1873, Edith wrote a short story and gave it to her mother to read. It was heavily criticised and Edith retreated to writing only poetry. Despite a child's need for a mother's approval and love, it was rare that she received either. This core relationship was indeed a troubled one.

By the time Edith was 15 she had translated a German poem "Was die Steine Erzählen" ("What the Stones Tell") by Heinrich Karl Brugsch, for which she was paid $50.

However her family did not wish to see her name in print (upper class women of the time only appeared in print to announce birth, marriage, and death). Consequently, the poem was published under the name of a friend's father, E. A. Washburn, a cousin of Ralph Waldo Emerson and a supporter of women's education and a great encourager of Edith's talents.

That same year, 1877, Edith had also secretly written a 30,000 word novella "Fast and Loose". Her central themes came from her experiences with her parents. She was very critical of her own work and would even write public reviews criticizing it. The following year, 1878, her father arranged for a collection of two dozen original poems and five translations, Verses, to be privately published.

In 1880 she had five poems published anonymously in the Atlantic Monthly, a much revered literary magazine. Despite these early successes, she was not encouraged to publish by others but did continue to write.

Edith was courted by Henry Stevens from 1880 and after two years they became engaged. A month before their marriage the engagement abruptly ended.

In 1885, at age 23, she married Edward (Teddy) Robbins Wharton, who was 12 years her senior. He was from a well-established Boston family, a sportsman and a gentleman of the same social class and shared her love of travel.

However this desirable match was blighted. From the late 1880s until 1902, he suffered acute depression. At that latter time his depression manifested as a more serious disorder, after which they lived almost exclusively at their estate; The Mount.

In October 1889 her poem "The Last Giustiniani", was published in Scribner's Magazine.

At age 29 Edith finally had her first short story published. "Mrs. Manstey's View." It had very little success, and another year was to elapse until she published again.

She completed "The Fullness of Life" following her annual European trip with Teddy. Burlingame was critical of this story but Wharton did not want to make edits to it. This story, along with many others, speaks about her marriage. She sent Bunner Sisters to Scribner's in 1892. The editor in chief, Edward L Burlingame wrote back that it was too long for Scribner's to publish. This story is believed to be based on an experience she had as a child. It did not see publication until 1916.

After a visit with her friend, Paul Bourget, she wrote "The Good May Come" and "The Lamp of Psyche". "The Lamp of Psyche" was a comical story with verbal wit and sorrow. After "Something Exquisite" was rejected by Burlingame, she lost confidence in herself.

By 1894 she had decided to write about her travels. This allied with her other interests of garden and interior design came to a publishing point in 1897 with a co-authorship on The Decoration of Houses, the first of several design books.

Her thirst for travel and to explore eventually meant some sixty trips across the Atlantic to travel across Europe and even Morocco.

Her husband, Edward, shared this love of travel and for years they would spend four, or more, month abroad until his illness deteriorated their quality of life such that they remained in America.

In 1888, the Wharton's and their friend, James Van Alen, took a cruise through the Aegean islands. Wharton was 26. The trip cost a substantial amount: $10,000 and lasted four months. Edith kept a travel journal during this trip that was later published as The Cruise of the Vanadis, her earliest known travel writing.

In 1901, Wharton wrote a two act play called "Man of Genius". This play was about an English man who was having an affair with his secretary. The play was rehearsed, but was never produced. One of her earliest literary endeavors (1902) was the translation of the play, "Es Lebe das Leben" ("The Joy of Living"), by Hermann Sudermann. "The Joy of Living" was a short lived Broadway production but was, however, a successful book.

She collaborated with Marie Tempest to write another play, but the two only completed four acts before Marie decided she was no longer interested in costume plays.

In 1902, she designed The Mount, her estate in Lenox, Massachusetts. Edith wrote several of her novels there, including The House of Mirth (1905), the first of many chronicles of life in old New York. At The Mount, she entertained the cream of American literary society, including her close friend, novelist Henry James, who described the estate as "a delicate French chateau mirrored in a Massachusetts pond".

Although she spent many months traveling The Mount was her primary residence until 1911.

With her marriage falling apart, due mainly to Edward's illness, she decided to move to Paris, living first at 53 Rue de Varenne, Paris, in an apartment that belonged to George Washington Vanderbilt II.

In 1908 her husband's mental state was determined to be incurable. In the same year, she began an affair with Morton Fullerton, a journalist for The Times, in whom she also found an intellectual partner.

She divorced Edward Wharton in 1913 after 28 years of marriage.

In 1914 Edith was preparing for her summer vacation when World War I broke out. Many fled Paris, but she moved back to her Paris apartment on the Rue de Varenne and for the next four years was a tireless, ardent supporter of the French war effort.

In August 1914 at the onset of War she opened a workroom for unemployed women; here they were fed and paid one franc a day. Thirty women started and this soon doubled to sixty, and their sewing business began to thrive. When the Germans invaded Belgium in the fall of 1914 and Paris was flooded with Belgian refugees, she helped to set up the American Hostels for Refugees, which gave shelter, meals, clothes and then an agency to help them find work. She raised and collected more than $100,000 on their behalf.

In early 1915 she organized the Children of Flanders Rescue Committee, which gave shelter to almost 900 Belgian refugees whose homes had been bombed by the Germans.

Aided by her influential connections in the French government, she and her long-time friend Walter Berry (then president of the American Chamber of Commerce in Paris), were among the few foreigners in France allowed to travel to the front lines. She and Berry made a total of five journeys between February and August 1915, which Edith described in a series of articles that were first published in Scribner's Magazine and later as Fighting France: From Dunkerque to Belfort, which became a bestseller. Travelling by car, they drove through the war zone; one decimated French village after another. She visited the trenches that were within earshot of artillery fire. She wrote, "We woke to a noise of guns closer and more incessant...and when we went out into the streets it seemed as if, overnight, a new army had sprung out of the ground".

During the war years Edith worked tirelessly in charitable efforts for refugees, the injured, the unemployed, and the displaced.

On 18 April 1916, the President of France appointed her Chevalier of the Legion of Honour, the country's highest award, in recognition of her dedication to the war effort.

Edith also kept up her own work during the war, which was now a prodigious output of novels, short stories, and poems, as well as reporting for the New York Times and keeping up her enormous correspondence. She urged Americans to support the war effort and to enter the war with its enormous resources of industry and men. She wrote the popular romantic novel Summer in 1916, the war novella, The Marne, in 1918, and A Son at the Front in 1919, (though not published until 1923).

When the war ended, she watched the Victory Parade from the Champs Elysees' balcony of a friend's apartment. After four years of intense effort, she decided to leave Paris in favor of the peace and quiet of the countryside. She settled a few miles north of Paris in Saint-Brice-sous-Forêt, buying an eighteenth-century house on seven acres of land which she called Pavillon Colombe. Edith would live there in summer and autumn for the rest of her life. She spent winters and springs on the French Riviera at Sainte Claire du Vieux Chateau in Hyeres.

Edith was a committed supporter of French imperialism, describing herself as a "rabid imperialist", and the war solidified her political views. After the war she travelled to Morocco as the guest of Resident General Hubert Lyautey and wrote a book, In Morocco, about her experiences. Wharton's writing on her Moroccan travels is full of praise for the French administration and for Lyautey and his wife in particular.

During the post war years she divided her time between Hyères and Provence, where she finished The Age of Innocence in 1920, which won the 1921 Pulitzer Prize for literature, making Edith the first woman to win the award.

Edith returned to the United States only once after the war, receiving an honorary doctorate degree from Yale University in 1923.

Edith included in her intellectual circle many of the great artists of her day; Henry James, Sinclair Lewis and Jean Cocteau were among her guests at the time. Theodore Roosevelt and Kenneth Clark were also friends. Of particular note was her meeting with F. Scott Fitzgerald, described as "one of the better known failed encounters in the American literary annals".

In 1934 Edith's autobiography A Backward Glance was published. This glossed over much of the problems in her life barely registering the criticism of her mother, her difficulties with Teddy, and her affair with Morton Fullerton.

On June 1, 1937 Wharton was at the French country home of Ogden Codman, working on a revised edition of The Decoration of Houses, when she suffered a heart attack and collapsed.

Edith Wharton died of a stroke some months later on August 11, 1937 at Le Pavillon Colombe, her 18th-century house on Rue de Montmorency in Saint-Brice-sous-Forêt at 5:30 pm. At her bedside was her friend, Mrs. Royal Tyler. The street is today called rue Edith Wharton.

Edith was buried at the Cimetière des Gonards in Versailles, "with all the honors owed a war hero and a chevalier of the Legion of Honor....a group of a hundred friends sang a verse of the hymn "O Paradise"...." She is buried next to her long-time friend, Walter Berry.

Edith Wharton – A Concise Bibliography

BOOKS
The Touchstone, 1900 (novella)
The Valley of Decision, 1902
Sanctuary, 1903 (novella)
The House of Mirth, 1905
Madame de Treymes, 1907 (novella)
The Fruit of the Tree, 1907
Ethan Frome, 1911 (novella)
The Reef, 1912
The Custom of the Country, 1913
Bunner Sisters, 1916 (novella)
Summer, 1917
The Marne, 1918
The Age of Innocence, 1920 (Pulitzer Prize winner)
The Glimpses of the Moon, 1922
A Son at the Front, 1923
Old New York: False Dawn, The Old Maid, The Spark, New Year's Day, 1924 (novellas)
The Mother's Recompense, 1925
Twilight Sleep, 1927
The Children, 1928

Hudson River Bracketed, 1929
The Gods Arrive, 1932
The Buccaneers, 1938 (unfinished)
Fast and Loose: A Novelette, 1938 (written in 1876–1877)

POETRY
Verses, 1878
Artemis to Actaeon & Other Verse, 1909
Twelve Poems, 1926

SHORT STORY COLLECTIONS
The Greater Inclination, 1899
Souls Belated, 1899
Crucial Instances, 1901
The Descent of Man & Other Stories, 1903
The Hermit and the Wild Woman & Other Stories, 1908
Tales of Men & Ghosts, 1910
Xingu & Other Stories, 1916
Old New York, 1924
Here and Beyond, 1926
Certain People, 1930
Human Nature, 1933
The World Over, 1936
Ghosts, 1937

NON-FICTION
The Decoration of Houses, 1897
Italian Villas and Their Gardens, 1904
Italian Backgrounds, 1905
A Motor-Flight Through France, 1908
Fighting France, from Dunkerque to Belfort, 1915
French Ways and Their Meaning, 1919
In Morocco, 1920
The Writing of Fiction, 1925
A Backward Glance, 1934

AS EDITOR
The Book of the Homeless, 1916

CINEMA
The House of Mirth (La Maison du Brouillard), a 1918 silent film adaptation (6 reels).
The Glimpses Of The Moon, a 1923 silent film adaptation (7 reels)
The Age of Innocence, a 1924 silent film adaptation (7 reels) (of the 1920 novel)
The Marriage Playground, a 1929 film adaptation (70 minutes) (of the 1928 novel The Children)
The Age of Innocence, a 1934 film adaptation (9 reels).
Strange Wives, a 1935 film adaptation (8 reels) (of the 1934 short story Bread Upon the Waters)
The Old Maid, a 1939 film adaptation (95 minutes) (of the 1924 short novella)
Ethan Frome (99 minutes) directed by John Madden. 1993,
The Age of Innocence (138 minutes) directed by Martin Scorsese. 1993,
The Reef (88 minutes) directed by Robert Allan Ackerman. 1999.
The House of Mirth (140 minutes) directed by Terence Davies. 2000.

TV

Ethan Frome, a 1960 (CBS) TV US adaptation.
Looking Back, a 1981 TV US adaptation of two biographies of Edith Wharton.
The House of Mirth, a 1981 TV US adaptation.
The Buccaneers, a 1995 BBC mini-series, starring Carla Gugino and Greg Wise.

THEATRE

The Man of Genius in 1901
"Es Lebe das Leben" ("The Joy of Living"), by Hermann Sudermann in 1902 - Translator.
The House of Mirth was adapted as a play in 1906.
The Age of Innocence was adapted as a play in 1928.